Praise for **The Great Reindeer Disaster**:

x **of delights** for both children and adults.'
New Statesman

'A sleigh worth of **humour**!'
Rebecca, age 9, *Times Educational Supplement*

'A **perfect stocking filler** of a book.'
Book Lover Jo

is book is packed with bucketloads of fun,
umour and is **awfully entertaining**.'
hloe, age 10, *Times Educational Supplement*

ique **and humorous** . . . An excellent
seasonal class read.'
Angela Kent, School Librarian,
Times Educational Supplement

About the Author

KATE SAUNDERS is a full-time author and journa[list?]
Her books for children have won awards and recei[ved]
rave reviews, and include future classics such [as]
Beswitched, *Magicalamity*, *The Whizz Pop Chocolate Sho*[p]
The Curse of the Chocolate Phoenix, Carnegie shortlisted
The Land of Neverendings and Costa Winner *Five Children*
on the Western Front. Kate lives in London.

About the Illustrator

NEAL LAYTON was born and raised in Chichester.
Whilst he was growing up he spent much of his time
playing in the dirt, making homemade catapults and
drawing pictures. He studied BA Graphic Design
at Newcastle, and MA Illustration at Central Saint
Martins. Neal now lives in Portsmouth with his family.

To Richard, who reads all my books
and even pays for them.

K. S.

For Dad and Charles Dickens.

N. L.

First published in 2020
by Faber & Faber Limited
Bloomsbury House,
74–77 Great Russell Street,
London WC1B 3DA

Printed by CPI Group (UK) Ltd, Croydon CR0 4YY

A CIP record for this book
is available from the British Library

ISBN 978-0-571-36112-0

FSC
www.fsc.org
MIX
Paper from
responsible sources
FSC® C020471

2 4 6 8 10 9 7 5 3 1

Trouble on
Planet
Christmas

KATE SAUNDERS
ILLUSTRATED BY NEAL LAYTON

faber

ONE
Pests

It was the week before the Christmas holidays, and something strange was happening to the Trubshaw family.

'I think we've got mice,' said Mum. 'I keep hearing funny scrabbling noises in the kitchen.'

Dad looked in all the cupboards and drawers. He climbed on a chair to look at the top shelf, he shone a torch under the washing machine, he checked the shed in the back garden, but he did not find the smallest sign of even one mouse.

'Maybe you heard something else,' he told Mum. 'I'll call Zappit just to make sure.'

Zappit was a firm of pest controllers. If your house had mice, or cockroaches, or any other pest, they put down poison to kill them.

The man from Zappit came – but he couldn't find any mice either.

'I don't understand,' said Mum. 'I know I heard something!'

'I'm sure there's a rational explanation,' said Dad. 'There's a rational explanation for everything.'

Mr David Trubshaw was short and rather fat, with glasses and curly hair, and he worked with computers. Mrs Judy Trubshaw was tall and skinny, with long blonde hair, and she worked part-time as a librarian. They had two children – Jake, aged ten, and seven-year-old Sadie. Jake was tall and thin, like Mum, and Sadie was small and round, like Dad.

Jake didn't care about the mouse drama. He was too busy looking forward to Christmas and making plans with his friends for the holidays.

Sadie thought mice were sweet, and if anyone

mentioned poison she burst into tears (she was always bursting into tears – Jake thought she did it to get her own way).

On Wednesday evening, when the Trubshaws were eating their supper at the kitchen table, they all heard something – a scratchy, scuttling noise, followed by a squeak.

'I told you!' said Mum. 'Now do you believe me?'

'It's in the food cupboard,' said Dad.

'I'll get it!' Jake jumped out of his chair and flung open the cupboard doors.

'Don't hurt it!' shouted Sadie. 'If you hurt that mouse, I'll poison YOU!'

The rows of tins and packets on the shelves looked completely normal – until Dad picked up a box of cornflakes and they all poured out through a large, jagged hole in the cardboard.

'That's been nibbled!' said Dad. 'We'd better call Zappit again.'

The man from Zappit came back the next day. He found no sign of mice, but left some little pellets of poison. 'These will fix them, Mr Trubshaw – one nibble, and they die in horrible agony!'

Sadie said her parents were 'evil mouse-killers'.

Another day passed, however, with no mice – dead or alive – and no more weird noises. The Trubshaws had almost forgotten the whole thing when Mum went into the kitchen and gave a loud squeal.

Everyone rushed in to find her leaning against the table, her face pale with shock.

'The fridge!' she whispered. 'Something moved in the fridge! I heard the bottles clinking together!'

'OK, I'll deal with this,' said Dad bravely. He opened the fridge, and this time everyone squealed.

It looked as if all the food inside had exploded. The

shelves were dripping with a great mixed-up mess of red jelly, chocolate pudding, yoghurt and soft cheese.

'I don't think mice did this,' said Dad. 'It has to be something bigger – a rat, or a squirrel!'

'Whatever it is, it's destroyed our food and made a disgusting mess.' Mum went to the sink and pulled on her pink rubber gloves. 'What if it's still lurking in there, and it leaps out and attacks me?'

'I'll prod about with a wooden spoon,' said Dad. 'Just to check. Stand back, kids!'

Jake watched as his parents took bits of ruined food out of the fridge, and suddenly had a feeling something weird was happening.

'Sadie!' he hissed.

'What?'

5

He grabbed Sadie's hand and pulled her out of the room. 'This isn't normal!'

'What?'

'Come on – people don't get squirrels in their fridges! This has got to come from you-know-where!'

Sadie's face lit up. 'You mean – Yule-1?'

Last summer holiday, the Trubshaw family had been whisked off to Yule-1, the planet owned by Father Christmas. They had made friends with elves and talking reindeer, Jake had learned to fly and it had been wonderful – but Father Christmas had wiped the memories of Mum and Dad, and only the two children remembered it now.

'FC said we'd go back one day,' whispered Jake. 'Maybe this is the first sign that he's about to call us, and I'll see Percy again!'

'Oh, wouldn't it be BRILLIANT?' Sadie whispered back. 'My human friends are OK, but I miss Belinda so much!'

Percy Prancer and his little sister Belinda were reindeer, and they had been Jake and Sadie's best friends during their time on the Christmas planet.

'It could happen any minute – remember how we were beamed up last time?' Jake wondered if he should sleep in his trainers, in case they were taken away in the middle of the night; he had missed his trainers on Yule-1. 'We'd better be prepared.'

* * *

Nothing else happened until Saturday morning.

Since the incident with the fridge, everything in the Trubshaw household had been completely un-magical. Jake and Sadie didn't mind too much because this was the day they were getting their Christmas tree, and that was always exciting. Mum went out to buy the tree and Dad climbed up into the loft to find the big box of lights and decorations. Sadie was playing a dancing hazelnut in the Christmas show at school and she practised her dance in the sitting room, while Jake played a computer game in his bedroom.

He didn't take much notice when something smashed downstairs, but a moment later, Sadie called out, 'Jake – come quick!'

'I'm busy!'

'Come **NOW!**' Sadie was waiting impatiently at the bottom of the stairs.

'What's going on?'

'Shhh – did you hear it?'

'You broke something in the kitchen,' said Jake.

'That wasn't me,' said Sadie. 'It was – something else!'

Jake caught Sadie's excitement. 'Dad's still up in the loft. It's either a burglar, or—'

Behind the closed door of the kitchen, something squeaked.

'Burglars don't squeak,' said Sadie. 'And it's too loud to be a mouse.'

Jake's baseball bat was on the floor under the coat pegs in the hall. He picked it up, in case he needed a weapon to tackle whatever lurked behind the door. Then, very carefully, he pushed the door open.

The kitchen was empty. Broken glass glinted on the floor. There were a few small toys scattered across the table, and nothing more.

Sadie took a closer look at the brightly coloured toys. 'Where did those plastic dinosaurs come from?

Are they yours?'

'Don't be silly, I haven't played
with toy dinosaurs since I was little.'

'Well, they're not mine,' said Sadie. 'I've never seen
them before.'

Jake went to the table and picked one up. It was
a stegosaurus, five centimetres long, and bright red.
'I don't think this is plastic.'

The tiny stegosaurus felt oddly soft and squidgy. He
squeezed it in his fingers – and then nearly jumped out
of his skin when the little creature suddenly wriggled
and gave him a sharp bite on the thumb.

'Ow – OW!' Jake shook his hand and the stegosaurus
dropped onto the table.

This was the most astonishing thing they had seen
since their adventure last summer.

The stegosaurus scuttled about on the table, letting
out a cry that was something between a growl and
a squeak. Two bright yellow T-Rexes came running

towards it. The two children stared in stunned silence as the little dinosaurs started to fight. They punched and bit, and their tiny, angry faces looked so funny that Jake and Sadie couldn't help laughing, though they did their best to break up the fight by pulling the creatures apart.

'These dinosaurs are really naughty!' giggled Sadie.

The weird little things were suddenly still again, like ordinary plastic toys.

'They must've come from Yule-1,' said Jake, looking at the tiny tooth-prints on his thumb. 'That's the only place where any kind of magic happens. But why are they here? I hope Father Christmas's computer hasn't gone wrong again.'

'I hope it **HAS**,' said Sadie. 'Then he'll need to bring Dad to Yule-1 to fix it.'

They heard Dad coming down from the loft with the box of decorations.

'We can't tell Mum and Dad about this,' said Jake. 'They don't remember, and they won't understand.' He quickly picked up the tiny dinosaurs and dropped them into one of the kitchen drawers. 'But wouldn't it be great if we got summoned again?'

TWO
An Old Friend

They did not have to wait long.

Christmas was only ten days away. Jake and Sadie spent Saturday afternoon decorating the tree with coloured baubles, tinsel and chocolates. In the evening, when the Trubshaws were in the middle of eating their supper, they heard the sound of rustling paper.

'The mouse!' gasped Mum.

'It's coming from one of the drawers,' said Dad.

The tiny dinosaurs had been quiet all afternoon.

Now they were thrashing about so violently that the whole drawer trembled.

Mum and Dad were scared, but Jake and Sadie were excited, and trying not to laugh.

'It sounds like a herd of elephants!' said Mum.

A loud squeak came from inside the drawer.

'I'm going in,' said Dad. 'I'll try to catch it.'

'Dad,' began Jake. 'You might get a bit of a surprise—'

'It could bite you,' said Mum. 'I've heard they turn vicious when they're cornered!'

'Oh, do calm down!' said Dad. 'I'll wear the oven glove, just in case.'

There was another loud squeak, followed by a noise that couldn't possibly come from a mouse.

Inside the drawer, a growly little voice shouted, 'You'Re a BUM!'

Another little voice shouted, 'No – YOU aRe!' 'Bum to YOU!'

And then there was more scuffling.

Mum and Dad were both thunderstruck.

'What on earth – ?' whispered Dad.

Someone knocked hard at the front door. In a daze

of astonishment, still wearing the oven glove, Dad went to answer it. A moment later he came back.

'I don't understand,' he said faintly. 'I must be dreaming!'

Out in the hall, they heard something that sounded like hooves, and into the Trubshaws' kitchen trotted an elegant young reindeer. 'Hi, everyone. Sorry to barge in like this, but it's an emergency.'

'**LUCY!**' cried Sadie. 'Lucy Blitzen!' Beaming with joy, she leapt out of her chair to hug the reindeer and cover her face with kisses.

On Yule-1, Lucy was famous. She was one of the flying reindeer who worked round the clock, every day of the year, to deliver the world's Christmas presents; they worked outside earth time so they could always deliver on Christmas Eve. The reindeer flew in squadrons, and each squadron had a different hat to set them apart from the others. Lucy wore a small bonnet of pale blue velvet, which was the uniform of the Janiacs (they called themselves the Janiacs because they liked novels by Jane Austen), and Sadie was a member of their fan club.

'Hi, Sadie,' said Lucy. 'Hi, Jake – Ginger sends his love.' (Her brother, Ginger Blitzen, belonged to another famous reindeer squadron called the Jambusters.) 'Don't worry about your parents. I've sprayed them with something to bring back their memories and it takes a few minutes to work.'

Mum and Dad had frozen like two astonished statues.

'What's the emergency?' asked Jake.

Lucy pulled a piece of paper from her saddlebag. She gave it to Jake and he saw that it was an advertisement for something. He read it aloud.

'We've got some tiny dinosaurs,' said Sadie. 'But they're not sweet and cuddly – one of them bit Jake.'

'And they can't stop fighting,' said Jake. 'Where did they come from?'

'They certainly weren't made at Father Christmas's toy factory,' said Lucy. 'He's banned them and he wants them all rounded up.'

'Why are they here, in our house?'

'Because of you,' said Lucy, smiling at Jake. 'When you came to Yule-1, FC put one of his magic microchips in your shoulder. The maker of those dinosaurs must have picked up your signal and put you on his mailing list.'

She used her mouth to pull something out of her saddlebag – a metal box with a spring lock. In one swift movement, the reindeer opened the drawer,

grabbed the dinosaurs and locked them in their tiny
metal prison.

'Phew!' she said, smiling. 'I think that's the last of
the little blighters!'

'This is a dream,' said Mum. 'Have I had this
dream before?'

'It's a talking reindeer!' said Dad, staring at Lucy.
'But there has to be a rational explanation.'

'You'll remember everything in a minute, Mr
Trubshaw,' said Lucy. 'As soon as we're in the shuttle.'

A flash of white light made them all cover their eyes –
and then everything went dark.

* * *

When the Trubshaws woke up, their kitchen had
vanished and they were in a humming, windowless box,
strapped tightly into their seats.

'Hey, we're back in FC's private space shuttle,' said
Jake, grinning at Sadie. 'WE'RE GOING TO YULE-1!'

'We're weightless,' said Sadie. 'Let's dance on the
ceiling, like we did last time.'

They undid their seat belts and immediately floated up to the ceiling.

'This is so cool!' Jake began to run around the walls.

'Look at me!' cried Sadie. 'I'm upside down and I'm doing my hazelnut dance!'

'Get back in your seats, you two,' said Dad. 'It's not safe to fool about in space.'

He grabbed Jake's ankle and Sadie's arm, and firmly pulled them back to their seats.

'Oh dear,' said Mum. 'I didn't bolt the back door—'

'That won't matter,' said Lucy. The young reindeer unfastened her harness and floated gracefully across the cabin to Mum and Dad. 'And you don't need to worry about your jobs, or the children's school – you'll

get back to your home at the exact same time you left.'

'I remember everything now,' said Dad. 'FC hasn't invited us for a holiday. Those ghastly little dinosaurs are a clear sign of trouble with the magic mainframe of the computer system, and he needs me to fix it.'

Lucy sighed. 'You're right, Mr Trubshaw; that's why FC is bringing you back to Yule-1. He's having terrible trouble with a certain mad inventor, who wants to make lots of your human money. He used to be one of the top inventors at the toy factory, but now he's working for himself – and he keeps having ideas for Christmas presents that are totally **BONKERS!**'

'Like those Titchy Tino-saurs,' said Sadie.

'Yes,' said Lucy, her furry face very serious. 'He made

them in secret, and he meant them to be really sweet so humans would buy them – but you saw how they turned out.'

'Those tiny monsters are horrible,' Mum said, with a shudder. 'All they do is fight and shout "bum". And they made a disgusting mess in our fridge.'

'The mad inventor doesn't have as much magic as he thinks,' said Lucy. 'His Tino-saurs haven't been tested by Father Christmas, or sprayed with Goodwill, and if you put them into a Christmas stocking they eat all the other presents.'

'What – all of them?' asked Jake.

'**NO!**' gasped Sadie.

It was terrible to think of coming downstairs on Christmas morning to find that all their presents had been chomped by miniature monsters.

'If FC has banned them,' said Dad, 'how did they get to earth?'

'The inventor found a way to hide them on one of the sleighs,' said Lucy.

'Is this mad inventor a reindeer or an elf?' asked Jake.

'A reindeer,' said Lucy. 'His name is Philpott Blitzen.'

'One of your family,' said Mum. 'It's coming back to me now! All you talking reindeer have the same surnames as the eight reindeer in that famous poem – "'Twas the Night Before Christmas" – you're all called Dasher, Dancer, Prancer, Vixen, Comet, Cupid, Donner or Blitzen! Is this Philpott a distant cousin of yours?'

'He's my uncle,' said Lucy, looking embarrassed. 'He's always been a bit of an oddball, but I swear he's not a bad reindeer at heart. Ginger says he must've got into the wrong company.'

All the Trubshaws cried out together, **'KRAMPUS!'**

Krampus was a hairy monster with the legs and head of a goat and a disgusting long black tongue. Hundreds of years ago, he had been employed to visit all the naughty children on Christmas Eve, and to put bits of coal in their shoes instead of giving them presents. Nowadays, however, all children were treated exactly the same, and Krampus had lost his job. He had been so angry that he tried to ruin Christmas, but Jake and Percy had helped to stop him in the nick of time.

'Krampus was a suspect,' said Lucy. 'But it's not

him – Father Christmas persuaded him to be good and now he sees that being good is more fun than being wicked. He lives in the attic of Father Christmas's head office, and he works as a tour guide in the Reindeer Waxwork Museum.'

'What about Nerkins?' asked Jake. Nerkins had been Krampus's wicked reindeer sidekick.

'He's turned good too,' said Lucy. 'He has a responsible job, and he's getting married soon. Philpott may be operating alone, and no one knows where he's hiding.'

'I'd like to talk to FC,' said Dad.

'He'll phone when you get to the office.'

'Won't he be there in person?'

'He's – he's away somewhere, at a secret location.' Lucy's face was suddenly shifty. 'I can't tell you any more.'

THREE
Best Friends

The space shuttle landed and the Trubshaws stepped
out into the bright sunlight of the Christmas planet.

'Oh, this is lovely!' said Mum. 'I'd forgotten that it's
always sunny here, and only rains once a month.'

'That's because Yule-1 has an artificial atmosphere,
and FC controls the weather on his magical computer,'
said Dad. 'I'm glad to see that the new weather app I
designed last time seems to be working.' His round face
was beaming – he was always happiest when he was

thinking or talking about computers, and (now that he remembered) he was proud of the work he had done for Father Christmas.

Jake and Sadie gazed around, too happy to speak. They had landed on the edge of a huge green airfield, where there were long rows of enormous, boxy sleighs.

'It's very efficient,' said Dad. 'People think Father Christmas has only one sleigh and one squadron of reindeer to deliver billions of presents to the whole world, and that's obviously ridiculous. It takes hundreds of sleighs, working round the clock every single day of the year.'

'My microchip's bleeping,' said Lucy. 'Excuse me – I have to join my squadron.' She rose up in the air and flew away as fast as a rocket.

The Trubshaws had seen squadrons of flying reindeer taking off on their last visit. Father Christmas rode in spirit on all his sleighs, so that he could deliver every single present himself, and he was very proud of the highly trained flying reindeer who helped him. Jake had learned to fly at his primary school on Yule-1, and he had even been part of a real

squadron pulling a real sleigh, but it was still an incredible thing to watch.

A crowd of elves in green uniforms had now filled one of the sleighs with sacks of Christmas presents. A bell rang, and Lucy and the other Janiacs – so pretty in their blue bonnets – galloped out of a big shed nearby. In a matter of seconds, the elves fastened the reindeer into their harnesses, and the sleigh zoomed into the sky with a mighty **WHOOSH** and a shower of sparks.

Sadie jumped and waved, and shouted, 'Hooray! Go, Janiacs!'

'My hands and feet are tingling,' said Jake.

'JAKE!' Mum cried. 'Oh dear – I forgot about your flying – come down at once!'

'Sorry,' said Jake. 'I didn't know I was doing it.' Without realising, he had whizzed up into the air, and he had to concentrate to get himself back to the ground. He was so overjoyed to be flying again that he couldn't help trying out a few swoops and turning a flashy somersault in mid-air.

'Show-off!' said Sadie, who was too little for school flying lessons.

A car with an open top pulled up beside them. The driver was an elf in a suit and tie. He was very small, about the same height as Sadie, and he had big, papery, transparent ears, like the wings of a moth. On their first visit the Trubshaws had been startled to meet the elves who lived with the reindeer on Yule-1, but they were used to them now, and this was an elf they knew well – Tolly Blobb, Father Christmas's personal assistant.

'Welcome back!' said Tolly Blobb. 'FC says he's very grateful to you all for coming.'

'We don't mind!' said Jake.

'Hi, Tolly,' said Dad. 'When will we see FC? Where is he?'

'I can't tell you yet, I'm afraid,' said the elf, his big bright green eyes very serious. 'He couldn't come to meet you himself – but your friends are waiting for you.'

The arrivals lounge was one of the square white buildings on the other side of the great airfield. The Trubshaws climbed into the car (it was rather a tight squeeze for Mum and Dad, who were so much bigger than elves and reindeer), and Tolly Blobb drove them across the grass.

They went through the door to arrivals (only Sadie was small enough to walk through it without bending down), and a neighing, growly voice shouted, **'JAKE!'**

It was Percy Prancer, the little reindeer who was Jake's best friend.

'PERCY!' cried Jake, giving him a hug. 'How are you, mate?'

'It's so great to see you,' said Percy, beaming all over his velvety brown face. 'I hope you have to stay here for months and months! I've got a new computer game – "Delivery Wars 4, Parcels of Doom"!'

Sadie rushed to hug Percy's little sister Belinda, and the two seven-year-olds did the secret hand-and-hoofshake they had invented last time.

'It's so nice to see you!' Mrs Prancer stood up on her hind legs to kiss Mum with her furry muzzle. 'Ron couldn't get away from his work in the sewers, but you'll see him later.' (Ron was her husband, father of Percy and Belinda.) 'We'll be neighbours again – your tent is ready in the big field next to our stable in Poffle Glen.'

'Oh, good!' said Mum. 'I've missed Poffle Glen, and our luxury tent.' On their last visit to Yule-1, Father Christmas had made the Trubshaws a lovely house in a red-and-white-striped circus tent – the only tent that was big enough for a family of humans.

A small, fat reindeer with a big, rather silly smile trotted over from the direction of the food court. His saddlebag bulged with reindeer snacks. 'Hi, Jake! Have a chomp-nut.'

'Fred!' Jake burst out laughing and felt such a surge of happiness that he shot a few metres into the air by mistake (his flying was still a bit shaky). 'How are you?'

It was Fred Dancer, one of Percy's best friends.

'Fred's staying with us at the moment,' said Mrs Prancer. 'His parents are away in the mountains, having a restful holiday in a health spa.'

'It's called Wobblin Manor,' said Fred cheerfully. 'They went there to get fit – my dad got so heavy that he kept breaking chairs.' Mr and Mrs Dancer owned a factory that made a popular brand of tinned moss, and they were both enormous. 'I miss them a lot, but staying with the Prancers is fantastic.'

'Thank you, dear,' said Mrs Prancer. 'Don't clog up your new brace with chomp-nuts.'

'I've got a brace on my teeth now, to make them grow straight – look!' Fred stretched his mouth into a

grin and showed off the gleaming
metal on his big and rather goofy
reindeer teeth.

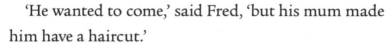

'Nice,' Jake said politely, trying
not to laugh. 'How's Eric – is he
here too?'

Eric Splatt, Percy's other close
friend, was an elf.

'He wanted to come,' said Fred, 'but his mum made
him have a haircut.'

'Guess what, Jake, I was top in all the flying exams,'
said Percy. 'Thanks to you and all the lessons you gave
me, when you were here last time. I bet you missed
flying when you got home.'

'Yes – but it wasn't as bad as I thought,' said Jake.
'And I didn't want to fly without you.'

'Come along, boys!' called Dad. 'Our coach is
outside; we're going home to our circus tent, where
Father Christmas will contact us by phone.'

An open-topped coach was waiting for them. It was too
small for the four Trubshaws and all their reindeer friends.

'Me and Jake can fly,' said Percy eagerly. 'Then you'll

have plenty of room.'

Jake was itching to try a proper flight, and didn't wait for grown-up permission. He took a deep breath, jumped into the air and felt himself soaring towards the sky.

'Mind the sleighs!' called Dad, far below. 'Stay well away from the flight paths!'

It was beyond brilliant. Jake and Percy flew gracefully through the warm, windless air of Yule-1. Jake knew that half of the planet was covered with huge sheds

and factories, where all the world's Christmas presents were processed. The part they were flying over, however, was all fields and flowers, and looked very pretty in the sunshine. At first they flew over green countryside, then they came to the town – the only town on the planet – where the elves and reindeer lived, and where the houses and shops were painted every colour of the rainbow. They were very careful to keep well below the flight paths. Sleighs took off every two minutes and were faster than the wind.

After half an hour of steady flying, Jake and Percy stopped for a rest in the middle of the town. They landed on top of a tall office building, so high up that they could look down on the roof of the building next door.

'That's FC's head office,' said Percy.

The roof of head office was flat and empty, with a door on one side, a large heap of rubbish on the other and a washing line. The door opened and a large, sooty, hairy creature walked out, carrying a big basket.

Jake and Percy gasped, for it was none other than Krampus – the monster who had nearly destroyed last Christmas. His long black tail dragged behind him and his goatish face looked very wicked.

'What's he doing there?' whispered Percy. 'I bet he's up to something terrible!'

'Krampus isn't bad any more,' Jake whispered back, remembering what Lucy had told them. 'He's got a job at the Waxwork Museum and he lives at head office. I think he's just hanging out his washing.'

Krampus's washing seemed to be a collection of filthy black rags. Jake and Percy watched, shaking with silent laughter, as he pegged them on the washing line.

There was something so funny about evil laundry.

When he had finished, Krampus stomped back indoors on his shaggy, goatish legs.

He came out again almost at once, carrying a big, steaming bowl of something dark and sloppy.

'Yuck,' said Jake. 'Now what's he doing?'

Krampus went to the heap of rubbish. 'Food!' he grunted.

'Someone's living in that heap!' hissed Percy.

The steaming bowl disappeared into the rubbish.

'Turnips and gravy **AGAIN**?' snapped a voice.

'Get back to work,' said Krampus. 'You said you'd make me one of those magic vitamin-shakes!'

'I'm too weak!' said the voice.

'Too **LAZY**!' snarled Krampus. He looked up sharply, his yellow eyes gleaming. 'We're being watched!'

Jake and Percy froze, terrified of being seen. Krampus had once been brilliant at flying, but he did not fly now. He only frowned and turned back to the door.

'Wait!' yelled the cross voice in the rubbish. 'Who's watching us – and why aren't you chasing them?'

'I can't,' growled Krampus. 'FC took away my power of flight. It was part of my punishment for trying to spoil Christmas. I won't be allowed to fly again for another six months.'

'You're supposed to be hiding me!' The heap of rubbish shifted and a head poked out – the head of a tatty old reindeer with a patch over one eye. 'I'm the most wanted reindeer on the planet!'

Percy nudged Jake and the two of them flew away as quickly and quietly as possible.

'I know who that is,' said Percy, quivering with excitement, as soon as they were far enough away to talk. 'The most wanted reindeer on the planet – it's got to be Philpott!'

'And Krampus is helping him,' said Jake. 'He hasn't turned good after all.'

FOUR
Trouble at Wobblin Manor

'We must report this to the police,' said Percy.

'Good idea,' said Jake. 'We'll do it as soon as we get home.'

'NO - NOW!' The small reindeer took a sharp dive down to the ground.

'Wait for me!' Jake's flying skills had mostly come back to him, but his landing was still a little rusty, and he only just missed falling on top of Percy. 'Ouch – sorry!'

'Hurry up!' cried Percy, almost dancing with impatience.

The two friends had come down in a busy street that was filled with shops and cafes, and crowded with reindeer and elves who stared at Jake, the tall human in his outlandish human clothes. Halfway down the street was a police station. Percy rushed inside, tripping over his hooves in his eagerness to report the criminals. Jake followed more slowly because the door was small and he had to take care not to bang his head.

There was a reindeer sergeant sitting at a desk, slurping tea from a metal bucket. He listened politely to Percy's rather garbled report – until he heard the name 'Philpott', and then he jumped out of his chair so fast that he spilled his tea.

'INSPECTOR!' he shouted. 'WE've got a lead on PHILPOTT!'

The quiet police station was suddenly crowded with shouting, neighing reindeer, all talking at once and bumping into each other. Jake couldn't help thinking they were rather bad at police work – but there was no crime on this planet, so maybe it wasn't surprising that they didn't know what to do.

Percy and Jake had to tell their story several times, and were only allowed to leave when Jake told them he had to get home for FC's phone call. Darkness was falling when the two friends set off, and the air was filled with the wailing of police sirens. Police cars packed with elves zoomed past them and flying reindeer police whizzed over their heads.

Jake had done a lot of flying and he was very tired. He kept yawning, and every time he yawned he lost height, like an old helium balloon.

'I hope I haven't missed FC's call,' he said to Percy.

'Don't worry,' said Percy. 'We're just coming in to Poffle Glen.'

Poffle Glen was a pretty place on the very edge of the town. There were parks and trees, playgrounds and cafes, and brightly painted houses surrounded by flowers. It had been Jake's home for several months last year, and he was very happy to see the large, red-and-white-striped circus tent again. It was in a field next to Percy's stable, and all the Prancers and Trubshaws came outside to welcome the two friends as they landed on the grass.

'We've been so worried!' cried Mrs Prancer, hugging Percy with her front legs. 'But then a police officer popped in to explain what you'd been up to – and we were even more worried!'

'You might have been hurt, or kidnapped!' cried Mum, hugging Jake. 'You should have flown away the minute you saw them!'

'No need to make a fuss,' said Mr Prancer. 'They both look fine to me.'

'You boys did exactly the right thing,' said Dad. 'What's the matter, Jake?'

'Your clothes!' Jake was laughing. 'I'd forgotten about your elf suit!'

Dad was dressed as an enormous elf, in bright red trousers and a bright green top with a big red collar. On his feet were green elf boots. Silliest of all, he wore a pointed red-and-green hat.

'It's very comfortable,' said Dad. 'I wish I could wear it to the office back on earth!'

'I **LOVE** my elf suit!' said Sadie, who had also changed. 'It's pink and purple – my favourite colours!'

'FC's going to call us later on his special government line,' said Mum. 'He's at a secret hideout in the mountains.'

This sounded a bit odd to Jake. 'But he's magic! I mean, this entire planet belongs to him and he can do anything he likes – so why doesn't he just fly over here to see us? Why does he need to make phone calls?'

'Maybe it's something to do with security,' said Dad.

'Before your call from FC comes in,' said Mrs Prancer, 'would it be all right for Fred to call his parents on that government line? They're up in the mountains too, at their health spa, and we can't get through on our ordinary phones.'

'I'm sure that's fine!' said Dad kindly. 'Give me the number, Fred.'

'Thanks, Mr Trubshaw,' said Fred. He took a scrap of paper from his collar and gave it to Dad.

The phone had been set up so that they could all hear every word crackling out of a speaker.

Dad pressed in the numbers and a distant phone rang.

A voice said, 'Wobblin Manor.'

'I want to speak to Mr and Mrs Dancer, please,' said Fred. 'In Suite Twelve.'

'Putting you through, sir.'

'Yes – who is that?' It was the voice of Mrs Dancer, and she sounded agitated. 'Is that my darling baby pooh-cake?'

'Hi, Mum!' said Fred. 'Hi, Dad!'

A deep reindeer voice in the background said,

'Hello, Fred.'

'I tried to ring you but your phones were switched off.'

'I'm so sorry, my precious!' said Mrs Dancer. 'There's some sort of VIP staying here and the security is ridiculous. I've had enough of this place and I wanted to leave today, but they wouldn't let me because of the— What do you think you're doing? Give me back that—'

The line went dead.

'Don't worry, Fred,' Mrs Trubshaw said, patting the stout little reindeer. 'It's probably down to that VIP – some bigwig who doesn't want people to know they're at a health farm.'

The speaker crackled loudly.

'Shh – it's FC calling us now,' said Dad.

There was more crackling, and then a high elf voice said, 'You're through to Wobblin Manor.'

'What? This must be a mistake,' said Dad.

'AHEM!' A loud cough came through the speaker.

'You seem to have found my secret hideout!'

'It's FC!' cried Fred. 'Hello, FC – you're at Wobblin Manor too!'

'I didn't want anybody to know I was at a health spa trying to get fit,' said FC. 'People expect me to be a bit cuddly – nobody wants a skinny Father Christmas – but I was getting so big that I was bursting out of my best red clothes. Are Jake and Percy there?'

'Yes!' neighed Percy.

'Hi, FC,' said Jake.

'I heard about how you spotted the idiotic Philpott hiding out with Krampus. You both did very well – thank you.'

'If you've locked them up,' said Jake, 'does that mean you don't need us any more?' This was an awful thought – it would be so disappointing to go home now, when he had only just begun to enjoy himself.

'Not at all! I need all the help I can get,' said FC. His voice was cross now. 'That nutty old reindeer managed to escape before my police could lock him up. They're not very good at catching people – they mainly deal with traffic. The fact is that I don't know the half of what Philpott's been up to – all his inventions look fine at first, and then they go horribly wrong. I should never have shut myself away in this place! Now I can't come back – and that's Philpott's fault too!'

'Excuse me, FC,' said Dad. 'Why can't you come back? You called me here to help, and I'd do it a lot better if you were in charge at head office.'

Father Christmas let out a long sigh. 'I'd love to come back – but it's impossible. You see, I took a a new vitamin-shake invented by Philpott. It turned out to have a terrible side effect.'

'What was it?' asked Jake.

'I'd rather not say. Everyone here at Wobblin Manor drank that vitamin-shake, and now we're stuck here until the side effect wears off.'

'My mum and dad!' Fred turned pale underneath his fur. 'What's happened to them – are they ill?'

'No, no, it's nothing dangerous,' said FC. 'It's just that we've all turned **BLUE** – and whoever heard of a blue Father Christmas?'

FIVE
Blue Christmas

It was great to wake up on Yule-1 the next morning.
Jake opened his eyes and was so happy to remember
where he was that he flew to the top of the circus tent
while he was still half asleep. The inside of the tent
was divided up into different rooms, and Jake liked
his bedroom here almost as much as he liked the one
at home. There was a comfortable bed, a desk and
chair, a duvet patterned with holly and a poster of the
Jambusters.

The only downside was that the walls were not proper walls. Everyone could hear everyone else. Jake woke up properly when he heard Sadie talking to Mum in the kitchen.

'Me and Belinda have invented a lovely new game. I can't tell you what it is because it's a secret and I have to fetch Belinda **NOW**.'

'It's too early,' said Mum. 'You'd better wait till after breakfast.'

Jake floated back to the ground and quickly got dressed (he was very glad to have his trainers with him this time).

In the kitchen he found toast and jam and a big jar of peanut butter.

'FC sent us some human food from his private supply,' said Dad. 'He knows how much I like peanut butter. He also gave me this rather primitive mobile phone.' The chunky phone beside his plate bleeped with a text message, and when he read it, he frowned. 'This is serious. FC has returned in secret, and now he wants me at head office immediately, but how am I supposed to get there? The buses round here take ages!'

'You'd better call him back,' said Mum. 'He's forgotten that you can't fly.'

'Hey – I can fly,' said Jake eagerly. 'I'll give you a lift.'

'You'll never get me off the ground,' said Dad.

'I bet I can, if Percy helps me.'

'Huh – you're just showing off,' said Sadie crossly. 'It's so unfair that I can't have flying lessons till I'm nine.'

'It doesn't sound very safe,' said Mum, looking worried. 'What if he's too heavy?'

'Let's give it a try,' said Dad. 'I've always fancied flying.'

Jake ran across the grass to the stable to fetch Percy, and the two friends tugged Dad a few metres into the air. They had never tried flying with a heavy load, but it turned out to be quite easy – like pulling something through water. To make sure he didn't fall, Dad tied one of his hands to Jake's hand and the other to Percy's hoof. Jake carried Dad's briefcase in his other hand and they soared into the air.

'Wow – this is brilliant!' yelled Dad.

'Don't drop him!' cried Mum.

Flying was the fastest way to get around the only town on Yule-1. Poffle Glen was miles away from the

centre, but they landed in front of head office in twenty minutes. Head office was the largest, grandest, most important-looking building in the business district. Jake remembered that Krampus had been living on the roof, and wondered where he was now.

'Thanks, boys!' said Dad breathlessly. 'Phew – my legs are a bit wobbly, but I'm still in one piece!'

Though Jake and Percy had been here before, they were still impressed by the entrance hall, with its red-and-green holly wallpaper and portraits of important elves and reindeer.

Tolly Blobb was waiting for them.

'Hi, Tolly,' said Dad. 'We're having a meeting with—'

'Shhh!' The elf put a spindly finger to his lips. 'Nobody knows he's back!'

'Well, I can't say I blame him for keeping it quiet,' said Dad. 'I'd be embarrassed about going to work if my face had suddenly turned—'

'**SHHHH!**' hissed Tolly Blobb. 'That's a state secret, and you mustn't mention it.'

He led them up the stairs and along a corridor, and knocked on the door of Father Christmas's private office.

'Go away!' cried a deep voice inside. 'I'm not here!'

'It's Blobb, sir.'

'Oh – all right, come in.'

Jake had met the great man on his last visit to Yule-1 and he was excited now – how many people could say they knew the real Father Christmas?

When they went into the office, however, FC was nowhere to be seen. A large folding screen stood in front of his desk.

'Good morning, FC,' said Dad. 'It's me – David Trubshaw – and I've brought Jake and Percy.'

'Good morning,' said Father Christmas, from behind the screen.

They all sat down on the row of chairs in front of the screen.

'Thank you for coming,' said FC's voice. 'My police aren't used to criminals and I need some help with catching Philpott.'

'Excuse me, FC,' said Dad boldly. 'Don't you think this would be easier if we could see you?'

'No!' groaned FC. 'I can't allow anyone to see me while I look like this.'

'We don't mind,' said Jake. 'So what if you're a bit blue? It's actually my favourite colour. I think it would look quite cool.'

'Father Christmas can't be blue.'

'Why not? You might start a fashion.'

'I have to look like the people I deliver to,' said FC firmly. 'I can be black or brown or white – but there are no blue people.'

'We don't care what colour you are,' said Dad.

'But if you're hiding, who's delivering all the presents?'

'I'm still riding on all my sleighs in spirit,' said FC. 'It's just that I hate looking like an alien. Even though humans can't see me, some animals can – a dog saw me the other day, and the sight of my blue face made him bark so loudly that he set off every other dog for miles.'

'Please come out, FC,' said Dad.

There was a long silence, and then FC said, 'All right – but you must never tell anyone about this. And please don't laugh!'

The screen rolled aside to reveal him sitting behind his huge desk. Father Christmas wore a grey suit and tie, like an ordinary businessman (he only wore his famous red suit on formal occasions). His hair and long beard were dazzling white against his pale blue face.

'Crikey!' said Dad.

'I should have known Philpott's vitamin-shakes were too good to be true!' FC said bitterly. 'They're called "Super-gloopies". Everyone at Wobblin Manor drank one. When we woke up next morning, however, we were all as blue as a Wedgwood tea set.'

'Does it last forever?' asked Jake.

'I hope not! I've got my boffins working round the clock to find an antidote.'

'This Philpott character's not very good at inventing,' said Dad.

'That's putting it mildly,' said FC. 'Every single one of his inventions has turned out to be RUBBISH, especially those Titchy Tino-saurs. And now he's sneaked hundreds of them to earth because he thinks he'll make piles of human money.'

'I suppose Krampus helped him because he wants to ruin Christmas again,' said Jake.

'No, no,' said FC. 'Krampus got involved because – well, I'll let you see for yourselves!'

He pressed a button under his desk. A moment later, the door opened and they all gasped aloud.

Krampus himself shuffled sulkily into the office. His shaggy black fur had turned bright sky-blue.

'Hello,' growled Krampus. 'I'm not trying to ruin Christmas now – **AND I AM NEVER SPEAKING TO THAT REINDEER AGAIN!**'

'All he wanted was to get into shape,' said FC. 'Just like the rest of us at Wobblin Manor!'

'I agreed to hide him because he promised to make me one of those Super-gloopies,' said Krampus. 'I drank it just before the police came, and all it did was turn me **BLUE!**'

'Maybe it'll wear off soon,' said Jake kindly, wanting to comfort the downcast blue monster. 'And it's not that bad. You look – er – fine.'

'Really? This blue makes my ears look **HUGE!**' For a hideous monster, Krampus was surprisingly vain.

He didn't exactly smile when Jake said he looked 'fine', but his scowl got a little more cheerful.

'Krampus is on our side this time,' said FC. 'He's sorry he allowed himself to be led astray – aren't you?'

'Yes,' snapped Krampus. 'I really am good now.'

'I'm afraid Philpott has been mucking about with my computer system,' said FC. 'That's why I summoned you, David.'

'OK,' said Dad. 'I'll fix it in no time – and I'll find Philpott. I know all your reindeer are microchipped.'

Father Christmas sighed. 'I've lost his signal. I have no idea where he's hiding.'

There was a knock on the door and two reindeer cantered into the office – Lucy Blitzen of the Janiacs and her brother Ginger of the Jambusters.

'Hi, Ginger!' cried Percy, beaming all over his furry face.

The Jambusters wore big moustaches, like RAF

pilots in the Second World War, and they were Percy's favourite squadron; he belonged to their fan club, the Junior Jambusters.

'Hi, Percy,' said Ginger. 'And Jake, it's great to see you back on Yule-1!'

'Thanks,' said Jake. He wasn't as mad about the Jambusters as Percy, but thought they were incredibly cool.

'You two are Philpott's only family,' said FC to Lucy and Ginger. 'You know him better than anyone.'

'He's the world's most embarrassing uncle,' said Ginger. 'We used to pray he wouldn't come to sports day!'

'I want you to think very hard about where your uncle might be.' FC pressed a button and a big TV screen rose up behind his desk. 'This is the only clue I have.'

A dark and shadowy picture appeared on the screen. It seemed to be a small room, like a garden shed. A weird-looking old reindeer was running backwards in a tight circle.

'Philpott!' said Jake. 'Why is he running backwards?'

'He thinks it reverses time,' said Ginger.

Philpott stopped, very out of breath. He was a bony, wrinkled old reindeer, with a black patch over one eye and a crazed expression in the other. Though he was old, he was wiry and strong, and moved surprisingly fast.

He glared into the camera. 'You'll never find me, Father Christmas! You'll never stop me selling my toys to the humans – I'm going to be the richest reindeer in history! You'll be sorry you fired me from the toy factory! It's time someone else got a crack at running Christmas! Give me control of Yule-1 – or **THE TITCHY TINO-SAURS WILL TAKE OVER THE EARTH!**' Philpott made a hideous face, and then added, 'Lucy and Ginger, if you see this blackmail video, please water my plants.'

The screen went blank.

Everyone was silent. It was dreadful to think of the Christmas planet being controlled by Philpott, and worse to think of the earth being invaded by Titchy Tino-saurs.

'Don't look so worried, Jake,' said Dad cheerfully. 'FC has hundreds of years of experience. He can easily deal with one nutty reindeer and a few toy dinosaurs.'

'Of course I can!' said FC, rather crossly.

'Water his plants?' sniffed Lucy. 'What a CHEEK!'

Dad took off his elf hat and sat down in front of FC's computer. 'I'll see if I can pick up a trace of his signal. Tell Mum I'll be home in time for supper.'

The sun was shining and the flight home was so much fun that Jake and Percy forgot to worry about Philpott and his threats. It was wonderful to be together again, fooling about in mid-air and making silly jokes. Jake had missed his reindeer friend.

And it was beyond wonderful to be flying again. Jake loved flying. He bounced along beside Percy, in warm air that was soft and springy like a mattress made of cloud, ridiculously happy. They had already decided to play 'Delivery Wars 4' on the big, chunky reindeer computer in Percy's bedroom.

When they got home, they found a large car outside, with blacked-out windows.

'It's my parents,' said Fred, outside the house. 'They've come to take me home, but they're too embarrassed to get out of the car.'

'It's because they're rather blue,' whispered Jake's mum, trying not to giggle. 'I begged them to stay for a bucket of reindeer tea but the poor things just couldn't bear to show themselves.'

'Thank you for having me, Mrs Prancer,' said Fred. 'Mum says she'll pop in when she's changed back to her normal colour. And I'll see you two at school on Monday – if you are coming to school again, Jake.'

'Definitely,' said Jake. 'I've missed Poffle Glen Primary.'

SIX
Class Outing

It was strange how quickly the Trubshaws got used to being back on Yule-1. Monday morning in the circus tent was a lot like a typical Monday morning at home. Dad went off to his work at head office, Mum went to her work at the reindeer library and Jake and Sadie walked to school in a chattering crowd of reindeer and elves.

'I'm SO glad you're back!' Percy told Jake happily. 'We've got a class outing this afternoon.'

'Where to?'

'The gift warehouse – a tour of the sorting shed and then tea in one of the canteens.'

'Great!' Jake had visited the enormous warehouse before, and it was a fascinating place; this was a million times better than the outings at his human school.

'Welcome back, Jake!' It was Eric Splatt.

'Eric – hi!' Jake bent down to high-five the little elf, who only came up to his waist.

'We're getting a new teacher this morning,' said Eric. 'A reindeer called Mr Comet.'

Poffle Glen Primary was a bright modern building, very like a human school except everything was smaller. Jake had grown since last time, and he felt very big and awkward in his tiny elf chair. He was wearing his elf suit today and though it was very comfortable, he was glad none of his human friends could see him.

'QUIET!' The new teacher trotted into the classroom. 'Good morning, everyone. My name is Clarence Comet.' He was a stern-looking reindeer in a collar and tie. 'I shall soon learn all your names – and I already know Jake and Percy.'

Jake and Percy gasped, **'NERKINS!'**

It was none other than their old enemy, Krampus's wicked reindeer sidekick.

'Call me Mr Comet, please,' said the reindeer formerly known as Nerkins. 'I've stopped being bad and trying to spoil Christmas. I've fallen in love with a gorgeous young lady named Primrose Cupid – doesn't that name sound like **POETRY?**'

Nobody in the class knew what to say, and they all stared blankly at their new teacher.

'Before I begin this maths lesson,' said Mr Comet, 'I shall sing you a song I wrote last night. It's called "Thank You for Not Laughing When I Proposed".' He coughed a few times, and then he threw back his head and started to sing, in a dreadful, tuneless voice:

'Oh, my beautiful PrimROSE!
Doesn't she have a wonderful NOSE?
She's the loveliest reindeer you could ever see,
And I can't imagine what she sees in a dreary
old twit like me!'

The whole class watched this performance in stunned silence.

'That's all I've got so far,' said Mr Comet. 'I'm still working on the chorus.' He picked up a book and smiled, as if starting a maths lesson with a love song was perfectly normal. 'Now please turn to page twenty.'

Jake nudged Percy and whispered, 'What's up with him? Is that how all reindeer behave when they fall in love?'

'No!' Percy whispered back. 'Isn't his singing terrible?'

'Jake and Percy, pay attention!' called Mr Comet. 'If you can't stop talking, I'll have to move you.'

This sounded much more like a normal teacher, and the rest of the lesson was a completely ordinary maths lesson. They all quickly put the embarrassing love song to the backs of their minds.

After lunch, the class got into a large bright red

coach (rather cramped for Jake) and set off for the enormous gift warehouse that covered half the planet.

Mr Comet gave them a lecture about it from the front of the coach. 'This is where the main work of Christmas is done. The humans wrap their presents, and those presents are magically processed so that Father Christmas can deliver them back to earth on Christmas Eve. As you know, this planet exists outside earth time, so we can **ALWAYS** deliver on Christmas Eve. It's a vast operation – the smallest mistake can ruin a whole Christmas.'

The coach stopped in a car park and Mr Comet led the class into one of a series of gigantic sheds, filled with miles of conveyor belts that made the whole building hum. Most of the workers here were elves – there were thousands of them.

'Gather round, please,' said Mr Comet. 'Your guide today will be Ms Primrose Cupid, the reindeer I adore. I must warn you that she is as fair as the rising sun – but here thou art, beloved!'

A lady reindeer trotted over to them and Mr Comet kissed her hoof.

Ms Cupid was a tough-looking animal, with a muzzle that was oddly long and thin, and sharp little eyes behind thick glasses.

'She doesn't look beautiful to me!' Jake whispered to Percy. 'Is that because I'm human?'

'No,' Percy whispered back. 'There's nothing the matter with her, but she's nothing special – even if you're a reindeer.'

'Clarence, stop kissing my hoof!' said Primrose. 'I've brought you a bucket of your favourite hot chocolate.'

'**My angel!**' cried Mr Comet.

Primrose lowered her voice so that only Mr Comet and Jake, who stood nearby, could hear her. 'Please don't sing any more love songs outside my house!'

'Didn't you like my midnight serenade?'

'My parents were in bed and you woke them up. Drink your chocolate.'

Jake watched Primrose as she picked up a small, steaming bucket and gave it to Mr Comet. For one moment he thought he saw her dip one hoof into the bucket and drop something into the hot chocolate – but it happened so fast that he decided he must have imagined it.

Mr Comet emptied the bucket with one mighty swig and turned back into a normal teacher.

'Stop talking! We'll be travelling on the indoor train – seat belts will be fastened at all times—' He whipped a hay-cake out of Fred's hoof. 'And **NO** food or drink!'

'That's **SO** unfair!' muttered Fred crossly. 'He's just had hot chocolate and we don't get tea for ages!'

Alongside the conveyor belts, the huge space was criss-crossed with the tracks of an indoor railway system, busy with little open trains that clattered past every few minutes. Everyone got into one of the trains. Ms Cupid stood at the front beside the elf driver, holding a microphone in one hoof.

'Welcome to the Warehouse Experience!' she boomed above the noise of the machinery. 'You're about to see the whole life of a Christmas present, from the moment it arrives here to the moment it leaves on FC's sleigh.

Please keep arms and hooves inside the carriage.'

Their train picked up speed until it rattled along like a giant roller coaster, and Jake was so excited that he didn't know where to look next – this was miles better than any ride in any theme park on earth, and the most Christmassy place he had ever seen. There was sparkle and glitter and dazzle, there were open carts laden with crackers, teddy bears and strings of lights. Crowds of busy elves trotted about with huge rolls of wrapping paper and bunches of holly.

'Wow!' he gasped. 'Last time we visited, we only got to see the sleigh workshop and that was pretty good – but this is **AMAZING!**'

'My dad works near here, in the Goodwill shed,' Eric said proudly.

'The what?'

'You'll see!'

Jake knew he was on a journey he would never forget. Every few minutes, the train stopped at another stage of the tour and Ms Cupid made a short speech.

'Here you see one of the soft-toy sheds in the toy factory sector.' A long, long conveyor belt carried an

endless line of cuddly pandas. A line of elves hopped and kicked beside the conveyor belt, and Jake couldn't think what they were doing until she explained, 'The elves are doing a traditional dance while they check the seams.'

Jake thought of his old soft toys at home, and the mountain of cuddly creatures on Sadie's bed. 'Excuse me, Ms Cupid, do they all come through here before they get delivered on earth?'

'No time for questions!' snapped Ms Cupid.

The little train started again, and got up to such a speed that the places they passed were a Christmassy blur of red and green and gold.

When they stopped, they were beside a huge wall of shimmering silver, like a sheet of stars. Jake saw painted signs: **'CAUTION – GOODWILL ZONE'** and **'MASKS MUST BE WORN BEYOND THIS POINT'**.

'This is where all outgoing presents are sprayed with a mist of Goodwill,' said Ms Cupid. 'The workers wear masks so they won't breathe in too much.'

'My dad says it makes them drunk,' said Eric, giggling.

'Stop talking!' called Mr Comet.

The train moved off, gathering speed – and then came to a sudden stop beside a grey building with no windows and a thick metal door.

'Oh,' said Ms Cupid, 'I don't know why we've stopped here – it's the Secure Isolation Unit, where we store anything that has been infected with Badwill—'

'Help!' screamed an elf's voice. 'Help-help-help!'

The metal door burst open and a terrified elf tumbled out of it – followed by something big and fierce and bright red, with a terrible growl and snapping teeth.

'That's the plastic stegosaurus that bit me!' cried Jake. 'But how did it get so BIG?'

The tiny toy – once small enough to fit inside the kitchen drawer – was now the size of an elephant. The large red dinosaur opened its mouth, gave a loud growl and yelled, **'BUM!'**

A siren went off and a crowd of security elves appeared out of nowhere. They climbed all over the plastic beast and sprayed something in its nostrils. It made an angry noise, as loud as a foghorn, and slowly collapsed to the ground.

'Calm down, everybody!' called Mr Comet. 'The

emergency is over – **AARRGH!**'

The emergency was not over. There was a loud **POP!** The huge dinosaur changed into a puff of smoke and the floor was suddenly covered with dozens of tiny dinosaurs, squeaking loudly, shouting 'You're a bum!' and running about like a brightly coloured swarm of mice.

'**HAHAHAHA!**' roared a voice above them. '**TAKE THIS AS A WARNING, FATHER CHRISTMAS!**'

A weird-looking reindeer swooped down out of nowhere. While they all stared, he scooped up the dinosaurs and shoved them into his grubby saddlebag.

'Philpott!' Jake gasped.

Nothing like this had ever happened before, in the whole history of Christmas. The rebel reindeer flew off before anyone could catch him, and panic broke out. Reindeer and elves ran everywhere at once, falling over each other, neighing and shrieking with alarm.

And then more security elves appeared with something that looked like a supersized vacuum cleaner and quickly vacuumed up all the remaining Titchy Tino-saurs.

'Pull yourselves together!' said Mr Comet. 'It's all under control!'

Ms Cupid's voice was shaking. 'I have to stop the tour, so we'll go straight to the canteen.'

'Hooray!' said Fred. 'At last this outing's getting good.'

* * *

The news was all over the planet by the end of the day.

'I think Philpott is a very mean old reindeer,' said Sadie, frowning. 'Those dinosaurs are sweet and he shouldn't have stuffed them into his smelly old saddlebag.'

'They don't strike me as sweet,' said Mum. 'Look at the mess they made in our fridge.'

'It's disgraceful!' sighed Percy's mother, shaking her antlers. 'I don't know how Philpott dares to threaten FC!'

The two families, plus Fred (who always stayed with the Prancers after school, until his mother finished work), were relaxing on the grass in Poffle Park. The weather was warm and sunny, and Jake and Percy had just finished a lively game of flying football. They were now eating ice creams.

'Funny to think it's winter at home,' said Jake.

'Belinda,' said Mrs Prancer. 'Don't put your chocolate stick in your school saddlebag, dear.'

'I'm saving it for—' began Belinda.

'Shhh!' hissed Sadie, putting her hand over the small reindeer's mouth. 'It's a **SECRET!**'

'Don't take any notice,' Jake said to Percy. 'They've invented some silly new game. You know how Sadie's always doing that.'

'Maybe it's not so silly,' said Percy. 'Last time you came, they had all those pretend tea parties to make Krampus and Nerkins good – and they worked.'

'OK.' Jake had to admit this was true. 'But now she thinks she's got magical powers, or something, and she can't stop showing off.'

Sadie stuck her tongue out at her brother. 'You're just saying it's silly to make me tell you about it and I won't – so there!' She whispered something in Belinda's furry ear and they both started giggling.

Jake was about to argue with her when Percy gave him a nudge and said, 'Look – what's that?'

A large, billowing white shape was coming across the grass towards them.

'It's a moving tent,' said Jake.

'It's my mum,' said Fred. 'She's still quite blue, and she doesn't want anyone to see.' He finished his ice cream in one big lick. 'Thanks for having me, Mrs Prancer.'

'Fred – my darling little pooh-cake!' cried the moving tent.

And then there was a noise like a clap of thunder, and a great puff of wind that knocked Jake off his feet. After a few seconds of bewilderment he managed to stand up again, and then he helped up Percy, who was lying on his back with his hooves in the air. They both helped Fred, who had been blown into a nearby bush.

'Wh-wh-what was that?' gasped Fred. 'It's never windy here, in case the sleighs get blown off course!'

'It was too strong for a gust of wind,' said Jake anxiously. 'It felt more like something exploding!'

'**MY TENT!**' shrieked Mrs Dancer.

Fred's mother had lost her tent, and underneath it she looked like a squashy pale blue sofa. A little group of reindeer and elves gathered round to stare at her.

'Look – it's Eileen Dancer!'

'Bless my antlers, she's **BLUE!**'

'If this is the latest fashion, I have to say it doesn't do anything for her!'

Mrs Dancer was so embarrassed that she blushed –

which mixed with the blue to turn her a delicate shade of mauve and made the crowd even more curious. The fuss only died down when Jake and Percy rescued her white tent from the top of a tree and she was hidden again.

'Thank you, dear boys!' Mrs Dancer poked her head out to give them both a slobbery reindeer kiss. 'I've only myself to blame – I drank one of those nasty Super-gloopies.'

Two big reindeer in police helmets galloped across the grass towards them.

One of them asked, 'Is Mrs Dancer here?'

'Yes,' said the voice inside the tent. 'Can I help you, officer?'

'It's about your factory, madam,' said the police reindeer. 'There's been a **BURGLARY.**'

SEVEN
Burglary

'A burglary?' gasped Jake. 'But that's impossible – there isn't any crime on Yule-1!'

Mrs Dancer let out such a shriek that the white tent puffed out around her and flew away.

'My lovely tinned moss factory! What happened – where's my husband? Tell me he hasn't been hurt!'

'Is my dad OK?' Fred had frozen with half a bar of reindeer chocolate sticking out of his mouth.

'Nobody's been hurt, madam,' said the police

reindeer. 'But there's quite a bit of damage – you probably heard the explosion just now.'

'I knew that was an explosion!' said Jake. 'What's been stolen?'

'That's not clear at the moment,' said the police reindeer. 'There's too much mess.'

Fred gobbled up the rest of his chocolate and hugged his mother with his front legs. 'Don't worry, Mum!'

'Oh, my little pooh-blossom, you're such a comfort to me!' Mrs Dancer gave Fred a huge, slobbery kiss. '**WHO** has done this?'

'I bet it was Philpott,' said Percy.

'Me too,' said Jake. 'But – why?'

'That troublemaker!' Mrs Dancer jumped up furiously. 'First he turns me **BLUE** and now he's burgled our factory!'

The stout, powder-blue lady reindeer galloped away across the grass, too angry to care about being seen.

'Mum! Wait for me!' cried Fred,

galloping after her.

'Come on!' Jake gave Percy a nudge. 'He might still be hanging about – this could be our chance to catch him!'

'That would be so cool!'

They shot across the grass, flying a few metres above the excited crowd. (Jake couldn't help thinking it was a bit of a pity that the elves and reindeer on this planet were so quick to get into a panic – but maybe that was because they'd never had anything serious to panic about.)

The factory was only a couple of streets away, and they all saw the signs of this dreadful crime as soon as they were out of the park gates. The road, the pavements and the houses were covered with great splodges of black slime. It dripped off the lamp posts and plopped off the gutters. Jake decided to fly just above the pavement, because he didn't want to get the stuff all over his valuable human trainers. He had tasted the tinned moss and thought it was disgusting, but reindeer loved it – he saw several of them licking it off lamp posts, garden gates and each other's antlers.

Mrs Dancer gave another shriek of fury when she saw the state of her factory. The big sign outside, which said DANCER'S BLACK NORWEGIAN MOSS, was so coated with the oozy moss that it now said DAN – ACK – WEG – OSS. The massive brick building had a jagged hole in the roof and the tall chimney that let out the steam from the vats of boiling moss had been blown in half.

The inside of the factory was even worse.

'Gross!' said Jake.

The vast floor was a lake of gloop, so deep that it came up to the waists of the elf workers.

'**NORMAN!**' Mrs Dancer waded through the gloop to her husband's office.

'**DAD!**' Fred followed her, with just his head sticking out.

'Now, Eileen, no need to make a fuss,' said Mr Dancer, who was a calm sort of reindeer, even when covered in slime. 'We'll soon get this cleaned up.'

'We heard the bang!' said Fred. 'Are you OK?'

'Hi, Fred,' said Mr Dancer. 'Yes, I'm fine, and so are all the workers, but it was quite a shock – that

Philpott character came crashing through the roof and the next thing I knew, he'd busted the main vat in the cooling chamber.'

'Why did he do this?' asked Jake. 'What did he steal?'

'Well, that's the funny thing,' said Mr Dancer. 'He left the safe with all the money, and the only thing he took was one sack of a chemical powder called Ploof-23. We make it from a kind of mould that grows in the mountains.'

'What?' gasped his wife. 'He did all this for a sack of Ploof-23? What does he want that for?'

'I can't imagine,' said Mr Dancer. 'We only use it to stop the boiled moss smelling of farts.'

'It's a **DISGRACE!**' snapped Mrs Dancer. 'This is the **CHRISTMAS** planet, and FC's always telling us that Christmas is about more than expensive presents and fancy food – it's about kindness and goodness – and there's nothing good or kind about burgling my factory! I want to see FC right **NOW!**'

* * *

'I'm sorry about all this upheaval, Jake,' said Father Christmas. 'Please don't tell any other humans – it would be so bad for my image.'

'I don't think other humans would believe me,' said Jake. 'But what's going on, FC?' He couldn't help being worried when his Christmas on earth was so close. 'Can one criminal spoil everything?'

'Certainly not,' said FC. 'This is nothing but a glitch. I'm very sorry about your factory, Mrs Dancer. I've already sent a team to repair the damage, and you'll be back in business by tomorrow morning.'

'Thank you, FC,' said Mrs Dancer. 'And thank you for these lovely milkshakes and snacks. My Fred is a delicate little reindeer and he needs to eat CONSTANTLY.'

They were in FC's private office, where the desk was crowded with mince pies, chocolate logs, gingerbread stars and other Christmassy snacks for both humans and reindeer. FC paced up and down, looking very worried. He was wearing his most famous outfit – the bright red suit trimmed with white fur – but his face was still pale blue and Jake was glad nobody on earth could see him. You wouldn't want this man on a Christmas card.

'I've just come from Windsor Castle, NEXT Christmas Eve,' said FC. 'I was doing a little job for the Queen – she found a couple of those horrid Tinosaurs in her wardrobe! I thought I'd got them all, but Philpott sneaked them to earth inside a tin of mixed biscuits. It's all part of his plan to make piles of human money from his inventions – and to punish me because I sacked him from my toy factory.'

'Did they bite the Queen?' asked Jake.

'No,' said FC. 'She was very nice about it, but I was dreadfully embarrassed. Philpott thinks he can set himself up as my rival. He doesn't understand that my Christmas planet is not a money-making business – humans might make money out of it, but not ME! My Christmas is a festival of peace and light, and my job is to spread **HAPPINESS!**'

Jake hated to think what would happen to Christmas if Philpott was in charge. 'Isn't there anything we can do?'

'Lots!' said FC briskly. 'I shall find him in no time, and then I'll send him into therapy.'

'Oh.' Jake thought this sounded a little too kind, considering all the trouble Philpott was causing. 'Won't he go to prison?'

'There are no prisons on my Christmas planet,' said FC, with a very kind look on his blue face. 'And none of my magical creatures are really wicked – just silly.' He pressed a button under his desk. 'I've got my best people looking into it.'

A moment later, a very wrinkled, doddery old reindeer trotted into the office.

'Greetings, young people.'

Jake, Percy and Fred had met him before – it was Professor Rudolf, and Jake remembered that he got annoyed if you mentioned the well-known human song about him. The real Rudolf did not have a red nose; he was a brilliant scientist who had invented a reindeer nose-light for foggy conditions.

'I'll give you the good news first,' said Professor Rudolf. 'I've invented a medicine to turn you back to the right colour, once and for all.'

'Oh, thankyouthankyou!' cried Mrs Dancer.

'Well done, Rudolf,' said FC.

The professor gave them each a spoonful of bright purple medicine. Fred's pale blue mother instantly turned back to light brown and FC turned back to everyone's idea of how Father Christmas should look – like a healthy, jolly human, and not a sick alien. It made Jake feel better just to see him.

'The bad news,' Rudolf went on, 'is that Philpott had a special reason for breaking into the Dancers' factory.'

'All he took was a bag of Ploof-23,' said Mrs Dancer.

'No!' FC's newly pink cheeks turned deathly pale.

'Ploof-23 does more than eliminate farty smells,' said the reindeer professor sternly. 'It's a vital ingredient in the making of TURBO-CAKES.'

'Uh-oh,' said Jake.

Turbo-cakes were the special magic cakes that FC's flying reindeer ate so that they could breathe in space. Jake knew all about them because he had eaten one on his last visit to the Christmas planet, when he had helped to pull the sleigh. They were black and sticky and smelly, and he thought they tasted horrible, but reindeer found them delicious.

'You know what this means,' said FC, in a shaking voice. 'If Philpott manages to make himself a Turbo-cake, he'll be able to fly to earth – and if we don't find him in time, Christmas as we know it will be DESTROYED!'

EIGHT
An Uninvited Guest

'The Ploof-23 won't be the end of it,' said Professor Rudolf. 'You'd better give me a full list of ingredients.'

'The recipe is extremely complicated. Philpott isn't clever enough to make one himself.' FC had recovered his confidence. He stood up, big and strong and smiling. 'I'm the only person in the universe who can make a Turbo-cake!'

'Do you make all of them?' Jake had wondered where the smelly cakes came from.

'Yes,' said FC. 'I have a laboratory next to my bedroom and I mix up a new batch for my flying reindeer every night. There's a lot of magic involved – very difficult magic. But I'll put a guard on the door just to be safe.'

'Wait till I get my hooves on that CHEEKY reindeer,' said Mrs Dancer crossly. 'I'll make him sorry he stole from my factory! Come along, boys, you can give me a lift home.'

They left head office, and the three friends hefted Fred's mother into the air. (Fred was grinning all over his face because he was so happy that she was back to her normal colour.) The Dancers lived in a big and rather flashy stable opposite Poffle Park. There was a pond in front of it, with a stone statue of a reindeer, and Mrs Dancer was so heavy that they nearly dropped her into it.

'Thank you, boys!' The curvy lady reindeer kissed Jake and Percy. 'I hope I'll see you on Saturday, at my Freddy-Weddy's tenth birthday party.'

'It'll be really great!' said Fred, who had handed an invitation to everyone in the class. 'We're going to the Waxwork Museum – that's where Krampus works now – and then we're having a **HUGE** tea!'

'Mrs Dancer's very nice,' Jake said to Percy, when they were flying home. 'But aren't you glad our mums don't call us Jakey-Wakey and Percy-Wercy?'

Percy burst into neighing reindeer laughter, and they spent the rest of the journey calling to each other in silly voices –

'Thanks, PERCY-WERCY!'

* * *

The next morning, when they were walking to school, there were big posters stuck to every wall and tree – a sulky-looking picture of Philpott, over the words **IF YOU SEE THIS REINDEER, CALL THE POLICE!**

That evening, there was a special announcement on Yule-1 television about the Titchy Tino-saurs. 'These things are **NOT** approved toys. If you find any of them, please shut them in a secure container and contact the **TINO—SAUR HOTLINE!**'

'I still think they're sweet,' said Sadie. 'Father Christmas is supposed to be kind – why doesn't he try being kind to them?'

'Because they're such a nuisance,' said Dad. 'A bunch of them got into head office and ate FC's slippers.' He looked hard at Sadie. 'I don't care how sweet you think they are – if you see any Tino-saurs, I expect you to report them **AT ONCE**.'

On Saturday, the day of Fred's party, Mum gave Jake a parcel wrapped in glittery paper. 'I had no idea what to buy for a reindeer's birthday present, but Percy's mother was a big help and I popped into Blitzen Brothers on my way home from work. I hope Fred likes it – it's a knitted rasta hat, like the ones worn by the Reggae-Reggae Reindeer.'

'He'll love it,' said Jake. 'The 3Rs are his favourite squadron.'

The Trubshaws were having a late breakfast, which they often did on Saturdays at home. Jake had a bowl of cornflakes, Mum and Dad had fried eggs and Sadie was under the table eating toast and peanut butter. Belinda was under the table with her, and the two friends were whispering loudly.

'What are you doing down there?' asked Dad. 'And why are you hogging all the peanut butter? I thought you didn't like it.'

'I've changed my mind,' said Sadie. 'I need peanut butter for something **SPECIAL**.'

'Oh, here we go!' Jake rolled his eyes rudely. 'She means that silly new game she's made up.'

'You don't know anything about it!' snapped Sadie. 'It's a **SECRET**.'

'It just looks like rubbish to me.'

As far as Jake could see, the game was nothing but a lot of scraps of paper spread out on Sadie's

bedroom floor.

'This is odd,' Dad said, looking into the jar of peanut butter. 'FC gave us five of these, and this is all we have left!'

'That's because I ate it,' said Sadie quickly.

Jake thought she looked guilty, but he had more interesting things to think about. He had never been to a reindeer's birthday party before, he had never seen the Waxwork Museum, and he thought it would be a good chance to talk to Krampus – maybe he could give them a clue about where to find Philpott.

'You'll enjoy it,' said Percy. 'It's a lot of fun – do you have waxworks on earth?'

'Oh, yes, there's a place called Madame Tussaud's,' said Jake. 'Our gran took us last year. It's full of wax models of famous people, and they're so realistic that it's quite spooky – especially in the Chamber of Horrors, where they're all murderers.'

'We don't have any murderers on Yule-1,' said Percy. 'But there is a scary room called the Black Stable.'

'Cool!'

They flew to the entrance of the Waxwork Museum,

where Fred and his parents were waiting with a crowd of excited guests; the whole class had been invited to the party.

'My little birthday boy will open his presents at teatime,' Mrs Dancer told them. 'Just leave them on the reception desk, and we'll go and see the wonderful waxworks.'

'There's a waxwork of my dad,' Fred proudly told Jake. 'It looks just like him, except that it's a bit too thin.'

The chattering crowd of reindeer and elves surged into the first gallery of the museum. They gasped with delight when they saw the waxworks and Jake politely pretended to gasp too, though the truth was that he found them rather boring. All the waxworks were of famous reindeer, and if you are human, one reindeer looks very like another.

'Good afternoon, everyone!' called the tour guide.

'Hi, Krampus!' said Jake.

'Your fur looks nice now the blue's worn off,' said Percy.

The formerly wicked monster didn't exactly smile, but they could tell he was pleased. 'Thanks, Percy – it's nice to be properly black again.'

'The black does wonders for your figure,' Mrs Dancer said kindly.

'I've been working out,' said Krampus. 'I do an hour every morning at the reindeer gym.'

'Did you hear that, Norman?' Mrs Dancer prodded her husband's bottom with her antlers. 'That's exactly what you should be doing!'

'I told you, dear,' said Mr Dancer. 'I'm too busy to go to the gym.'

'Follow me, please,' called Krampus. 'You're allowed to take photos, but don't touch the exhibits.'

It was strange to see the once-bad monster as a museum guide. Jake stayed at the back of the crowd, partly because he was taller than everyone else and partly to hide his yawns. He liked the waxworks of the famous flying squadrons, such as the Jambusters and the Janiacs, and it was fun to see the wax version of Fred's dad, but there were endless rooms filled with wax models of reindeer he didn't know, and he was soon

very bored indeed.

Near the end of the tour, however, in a gallery of reindeer TV stars, he suddenly spotted something weird out of the corner of his eye.

'Percy!' he hissed into his friend's furry ear. 'One of them **MOVED!**'

Percy jumped up on his back legs to survey the room. 'I don't see anything but waxworks,' he whispered back. 'You must've imagined it.'

'I suppose so,' said Jake.

But in the next gallery he saw it again – one of the wax reindeer apparently moving. He only saw it for a fraction of a second, and decided not to say anything in case he ended up looking silly.

'We are now about to enter our **SCARIEST** room – the **BLACK STABLE!**' announced Krampus. 'Here you will see the worst criminals in the history of this planet!'

'But there are no criminals on this planet,' Jake pointed out.

'Well, there's the two of us,' said Krampus. 'Me and my old sidekick Nerkins.'

'You've both turned good now.'

'OK,' said Krampus, rather annoyed. 'You'll see waxworks of what we looked like when we were still bad. I'm happy to pose beside the model of me if you want to take photos.' He added, 'For a small fee.'

The crowd of reindeer and elves were silent as they went through the door of the Black Stable.

'This is CREEPY!' said Fred, shuffling closer to his mother.

Jake was very curious about the reindeer version of the Chamber of Horrors; the human version, at Madame Tussaud's, had frightened him more than he liked to admit. Once he got inside the Black Stable, however, it was difficult not to laugh. The room was small and very dark, and there were only three waxworks – Krampus, his old friend Nerkins and a shabby old reindeer with an eyepatch.

'Yes – it's a brand-new model of Philpott!' said Krampus. 'They like to keep up to date in this museum.'

He stood proudly beside the wax model of himself, and everyone took photos.

'It doesn't look much like him,' Jake whispered to

Percy. 'And I can't be scared of Nerkins now that he's our teacher. That new model of Philpott is the only one that looks real.'

Jake took a closer look at the very realistic model of Philpott, with its black eyepatch and shabby fur. There was something odd about it – he could have sworn it was staring at him.

'Isn't that marvellous?' cried Mrs Dancer. 'Norman, take a photo of us together!'

She went to stand beside the waxwork, but tripped over her hooves and fell right on top of it. 'Aargh!'

To everyone's amazement, instead of breaking under the weight of the portly reindeer, the model yelled, **'OUCH!'**

'That's not a waxwork!' gasped Jake. 'That's the **REAL PHILPOTT!**'

NINE
Sadie's Secret

The attack happened very fast. Philpott took a giant leap and landed on top of Jake. Before Jake could work out what was happening, the rickety old reindeer fastened his mouth on the back of his elf suit and dragged him through the nearest window.

Jake suddenly found himself dangling in mid-air, far above the street.

'Hey – what're you doing? Let me go!'

'Don't you dare drop him!' roared Krampus, leaning

out of the broken window. 'If you hurt that human, I'll shake you till your antlers rattle!'

Jake struggled and shouted and tried to fly away, but Philpott was too strong for him. He carried on flying – rather bumpily now – over the rooftops of the town, and dropped Jake behind a big chimney.

'Ow – that really hurt!' Jake sat up, shaking his head to clear it. 'What do you want with me?'

'It won't take a moment,' said Philpott. He clamped a bony leg across Jake's body to hold him down, and took something out of his saddlebag – a large pair of metal pliers, like the ones Dad used to pull nails out of floorboards. 'I'll let you go as soon as I've got it.'

'Got what?'

'Your tooth.'

'WHAT?'

'I'm going to pull out one of your teeth,' said Philpott. 'I need a human tooth and yours are perfect!'

He tried to stick the pliers into Jake's mouth.

Jake clamped his mouth tight shut and fought with all his strength. He was quite brave when he went to the dentist on earth, but it was truly horrible to think of having a tooth pulled out like this.

'Stop being awkward,' said Philpott. 'I only need one – **AAARGH!**' He let out a long, neighing scream, dropped the pliers and released his grip on Jake.

'Percy!' gasped Jake.

The little reindeer had swooped out of nowhere to give Philpott a tremendous bite on his bony old bum. Philpott thrashed and stamped, but Percy bravely kept on biting until Jake was properly free and back on his feet.

'POOH!' yelled Philpott. 'Tell PA CHRISTMAS he'll never stop me!' He flew off into the maze of rooftops and chimneys.

'That was brilliant!' Jake breathlessly hugged Percy. 'He wanted to pull out one of my teeth – you saved me just in time!'

'Why did he want your tooth?'

'I don't know and I don't care, but it would've been really painful!'

They flew back into the museum through the smashed window, and were rather embarrassed when everybody clapped and cheered.

'I'm sorry I couldn't help you, Jake,' said Krampus. 'But I can't fly yet. All I could do was call the police.'

'That's OK.' Jake found that he liked the old monster and wanted to cheer him up. 'You did your best.'

'Now we can get on with my Freddy-Weddy's party!' declared Mrs Dancer. 'But where is he?' She looked around frantically. 'What's happened to my little birthday boy?'

'I'm here,' said Fred's voice.

'Where?'

'On the ceiling – and I can't get down.'

Everyone looked up at the high ceiling and saw a blob of brown fur. Jake and Percy flew up to pull their friend back down to the floor.

'Thanks!' said Fred. 'I tried to follow you out of the window, but you know I'm rubbish at flying – I just turned upside down, like I did in my Grade Two exam.'

'My precious little pooh, what a shock you gave me!' Mrs Dancer hugged and kissed him. 'I need a good sit-down and a bucket of tea and my poor Freddy must have something to eat **AT ONCE!**'

'Don't fuss, Mum, I'm fine,' said Fred. 'Though I do fancy a slice of birthday cake.'

Everyone had been silenced by the shock of the attempted kidnap, but the word 'cake' reminded them that they were at a party, and they moved off to the cafe in a noisy, cheerful crowd.

'Sit down, everyone!' called Mrs Dancer. 'It's teatime!'

The birthday tea was incredible. There were two huge cakes, one for reindeer and one for elves and humans. There were sparklers, and a banner that said **HAPPY BIRTHDAY, FRED!!** in neon letters.

Fred opened his presents and he loved them all – especially the 3Rs hat from Jake, which he put on at once, over his antlers. 'Thanks, Jake! And Percy – thanks for the rainy-day hoof covers!'

The hoof covers were like four little red wellies, and when Fred put them on he looked like a cushion on wheels.

'Hoof covers are really trendy,' said Percy. 'I've got green ones.'

The birthday party ended with dancing, but Jake couldn't forget what had happened with Philpott, and in the middle of all the fun he borrowed Krampus's phone to make his report to head office.

'Thanks, Krampus,' he said when he had finished. 'I didn't get to speak to FC – I left a message with Tolly Blobb. Do you know why Philpott wanted one of my teeth?'

'Maybe he wanted to use it for one of his inventions,' suggested Krampus. 'Sorry, I can't chat now – I have to hand out the going-home bags.'

Worried as he was, Jake couldn't help laughing to himself at the sight of the horned monster giving out

the fabulous party bags of snacks, puzzles and games.

'Thanks for having us, mate,' said Jake, giving Fred a friendly pat. 'I hope all that Philpott stuff didn't spoil your party too much.'

'Spoil it? You must be JOKING!' chuckled Fred. 'That was the best birthday party EVER!'

* * *

Jake and Percy flew back to Poffle Glen full of party food and tired out with dancing and excitement. Both sets of parents rushed out to meet them when they landed.

'It's all over the news – that crazy reindeer tried to kidnap you!' said Dad, hugging Jake. 'Are you all right?'

'I'm fine, thanks to Percy.'

'Well done, Percy,' said Mum.

'Philpott wanted one of my teeth,' Jake told them. 'I reported it to Tolly Blobb.'

'Yes, Tolly called me about that,' said Dad. 'Philpott thinks a crushed human tooth is one of the things that goes into Turbo-cakes. He's totally wrong – but maybe you should keep your mouth shut when you go outside, in case he tries again.'

'You're just in time for supper,' said Jake's mother. 'If you've got any room left, after all that cake.'

'I've made some lovely boiled hay,' said Percy's mother. 'Jake, would you tell Belinda it's time to come home?'

'OK,' said Jake. 'See you tomorrow, Perce.' He high-fived Percy's hoof and went into the striped circus tent, which felt very welcoming and homelike.

'Those girls have been shut away in Sadie's room all afternoon,' said Mum. 'They've covered the floor with little bits of paper, and they've spent hours making a big green circle.'

'That's quite a noisy game they're playing,' said Dad. 'They've had the radio blaring out, ever since I got back from head office.'

'But Sadie doesn't have a radio!' Jake went over to his sister's bedroom. The door was only a tent flap, and there was a big sign in purple felt-tip – 'KEEP OUT!!!' He could hear strange growls and squeaks, like a crowd at a faraway football match.

'Belinda!' he called. 'Your mum says it's supper time!'

'GO AWAY!' yelled Belinda.

'CAN'T YOU READ?' shouted Sadie.

Inside Sadie's bedroom there was a sudden burst of loud, tuneless singing:

'Old Macdonald had a farm – bum-bum-bum-bum-BUM!'

And at the same moment, Dad let out a yelp of pain. A tiny bright yellow T-Rex had bitten his finger, and he couldn't shake it off.

'Where did that thing come from?' gasped Mum. 'I thought the dinosaurs had all been rounded up!'

'It was in the peanut butter,' said Dad. 'It jumped out at me when I opened the jar.'

He shook the little creature off his finger. The yellow T-Rex was covered with peanut butter, and it left tiny peanut-butter footprints as it scuttled across the kitchen table. It jumped down to the floor and slipped under the tent flap that was Sadie's bedroom door.

A chorus of rough, growling, squeaking voices shouted out –

'*Ha ha ha – where you BIN, you BUM?*'

'What's going on?' Jake pulled the tent flap aside, and Sadie's secret was revealed.

The floor of her bedroom swarmed with tiny dinosaurs. There were dinosaurs on Sadie's shoulders, and more dinosaurs strolled up and down her arms. There were tiny dinosaurs perched in Belinda's antlers, like decorations on a Christmas tree.

'Oh, you naughty girls!' said Mum. 'Those things are dangerous and FC gave orders to round them up!'

Sadie scowled. 'They're SWEET and it's not fair to round them up!'

'We found them under the sink in our stable,' said Belinda. 'And instead

of taking them to the police, we kept them to play with. There were only three of them at first – I don't know where all the others came from.'

'Don't they bite you?' asked Jake.

'No,' said Sadie. 'We've trained them not to.'

'One of them bit **ME!**' said Dad.

'That's because you scared it,' said Sadie sternly. 'You have to be very quiet and still.'

Jake knelt down on the floor to get a closer look at the Tino-saurs, privately thinking they were rather creepy. 'Have you trained them to stop fighting?'

'Of course,' said Sadie. 'And it's really easy. You just put a bit of peanut butter on your finger and let them lick it off.'

'So that's what happened to my peanut butter!' said Dad.

'We need it to control them,' said Belinda. 'We're training them to run races – just the T-Rexes, because they're the fastest. That big green circle on the floor is our racetrack.'

'Cool!' Jake was more interested now – he liked the idea of racing Tino-saurs. 'Which T-Rex is the fastest?'

'The blue one with the yellow dot on his head,' said Belinda eagerly. 'I gave him the chocolate stick from my ice cream and it made him super-strong.'

Jake looked down at the crowd of dinosaurs on the floor and easily picked out the T-Rex with the blob of yellow on his blue head; he was slightly bigger than the others, and his tiny face was fierce.

'I'll show you how I shut them up,' said Sadie, looking very pleased with herself. **'Dinos – SLEEP!'**

The dinosaurs instantly became still and silent. They fell off Belinda's antlers and flopped lifelessly on Sadie's duvet, like plastic toys.

'Wow!' Jake was impressed. 'But how do you stop them growing huge, like the dinos at the warehouse?'

'They only do that when they're frightened.'

'I'm sorry, kids,' said Dad, in his firmest voice. 'You

all saw the warning on TV. Anyone who finds one of these creatures must shut it up in a secure box and call the special Tino-saur Hotline.'

'NO!' cried Sadie. 'I won't let you!' She burst into tears and stamped her feet at the same time, which was a sign that she was very angry indeed. 'You're so MEAN!'

'I'll see Belinda home across the garden,' said Mum. 'And then I'll call the Hotline.'

Sadie made an incredible fuss, but her parents would not budge. Mum phoned the Tino-saur Hotline, swept the dinos up with the dustpan and brush and shut them in a large biscuit tin. Jake decided he was glad to see them safely locked up; the races might be fun, but he didn't like to think of the bitey little creatures running about in the tent and maybe hiding in his shoes.

'Phew!' said Dad.

'I can't believe how mean you are,' grumbled Sadie. 'You've ruined my best game and you don't even care!'

The doorbell rang and a voice called, 'Tino-saur Collection!'

Mum opened the tent flap and a reindeer trotted in with a large metal box – a lady reindeer in a white suit, with protective covers on her hooves and antlers.

'OK, I've come to take your Tino-saurs.'

There was something familiar about her thick glasses and long muzzle.

'Hey, it's Primrose Cupid!' said Jake. 'I saw you on our school trip – you're engaged to my teacher.'

'That is correct,' said Ms Cupid stiffly. 'Now I have to treat your house with a simple anti-Badwill spray. Are any of you allergic to fried carpets or roasted curtains?'

'I don't think so,' said Dad. 'We've never tried eating them.'

'Stand still, please.' Ms Cupid took a can from the pocket of her protective suit and sprayed the air around the Trubshaws. 'OK – hand them over.'

Mum gave her the biscuit tin and she zipped it into her high-security saddlebag.

'Where are you taking them?' asked Sadie. 'You can't put them in prison! They need lots of space to play and they like peanut butter – the smooth sort.'

Ms Cupid opened her mouth, but before she could say anything, a loud voice outside began to bellow a tuneless song –

'P is for PERFECT – my angel PRIMROSE!

R is for ROUGH – like the fur on her nose!

I is for ILLUMINATION – the light in her eyes!

M is for MINCE – her favourite pies!

R is for ROMANCE – she's queen of my heart!

O is for OH, NO – let us never part!

S is for SILLY – which she is never!

E is for ENGAGED – I adore her forever!'

'Sorry,' said Primrose, 'it's Clarence. I know he's a terrible singer, but I can't stop him doing his dreadful serenades – he follows me everywhere and I get really embarrassed.'

'I think it's romantic,' said Mum kindly. 'He's telling the whole world he's madly in love with you.'

'Yes, but—' The long-nosed reindeer was about to say something, but quickly changed her mind. 'I'll go and shut him up.'

A brass band started to play.

'Oh dear,' Primrose said, looking miserable. 'I begged him to stop hiring musicians! At first it was just one elf with a guitar but then it got completely out of hand and whole orchestras started turning up! Could you all do me a favour and not tell Father Christmas about this?'

'Why not?' asked Jake.

'I – I don't want poor Clarence to get into trouble. Excuse me—' Primrose hurried outside. A few minutes later the noise stopped, the musicians packed up and went home and Poffle Glen was quiet once more.

Jake remembered the class trip to the warehouse. He was now sure he had seen Primrose slipping something into Mr Comet's hot chocolate – but had she? He decided to say nothing to anyone until he could be certain.

'Goodness, it's late,' said Mum. 'You two should be in bed.'

'Me too,' said Dad, yawning. 'I've had a very long day working on FC's computer system!'

A moment later, the doorbell rang again.

'Primrose must've forgotten something,' said Mum.

But the reindeer at the door was not Ms Cupid. It was Lucy Blitzen, very out of breath and trying not to cry.

'I'm sorry, Mr Trubshaw,' said Lucy. 'I've come to take you to head office – this is a serious emergency. My uncle has **KIDNAPPED** Ginger!'

TEN
Dream-sneaker

'Ginger!' gasped Jake. 'I hope he's not in danger! And what'll happen to the Jambusters?'

'The Jambusters are grounded,' said Lucy. 'They can't fly without him.'

'Are you sure your brother is with Philpott?' asked Mum, kindly stroking her back.

Lucy nodded. 'Ginger disappeared just before his squadron took off, and Uncle Phil sent Father Christmas a ransom note. He says he won't let him go unless FC gives him the warehouse.'

'That's ridiculous!' said Jake. 'FC would never give him the warehouse! Why is he doing this?'

'It's those Titchy Tino-saurs.' Tears trembled in Lucy's eyes. 'You have to understand how angry Uncle Phil was when FC refused to let him make them. He still thinks the humans will buy them as Christmas presents.'

Even Sadie could see how dreadful this would be. 'But they'd eat all the other presents!'

'FC has searched every centimetre of Yule-1,' said Lucy, 'and he can't find a single trace of Uncle Phil or Ginger.'

'Does that mean he's got to earth?' asked Jake. 'I thought you said he wasn't clever enough to make Turbo-cakes!'

'He's not,' said Lucy. 'In the end, he got impatient and stole Ginger's ration of cakes.'

'Keep calm, everybody,' said Dad. He stood up and put on his pointed elf hat. 'We'll soon track him down – my computer system is a lot smarter than your silly uncle!'

* * *

It had been a very long and exciting day, and despite his worries about Ginger, Jake fell asleep as soon as he got into bed. He immediately began to dream.

In his dream, the inside of his head was like an old television with a dingy black-and-white screen.

The screen flickered and a fuzzy picture of Philpott appeared.

'Testing . . . testing . . .' said the seedy old reindeer. 'This is Philpott Blitzen testing the DREAM–SNEAKER . . . If you can see me, it means I've SNEAKED into your DREAM!'

'Dreams are private,' said Jake, inside his head. 'Go away.'

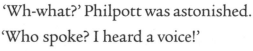

'Wh-what?' Philpott was astonished. 'Who spoke? I heard a voice!'

'Yes, you heard me,' said Jake. 'Get out of my dream!'

'Oh, my antlers!' cried Philpott. 'It WORKS! I can sneak into people's dreams!'

'I don't want to dream about you,' said Jake. 'For the last time, go away!'

'I can see you now!' Philpott looked directly at Jake. 'You're the human boy. What'll you give me to leave your dreams alone, human boy?'

'That's blackmail!'

'Any amount of human money is useful to me,' said Philpott. 'Your pocket money will do nicely.'

'I'm not giving you my pocket money.' The dream-Jake was calm. 'What do you want it for, anyway? You can't spend it on Yule-1.'

'Ha! I'm not on Yule-1 – so there!'

'Are you on earth?'

'Not telling!' shouted Philpott. 'Give me your money!'

'No!'

'If you don't, you'll dream about me every single night, and they won't be nice dreams like this one.' Philpott clapped his front hooves together and the scenery of Jake's dream suddenly changed.

He stood on a bleak hillside, very steep and covered with big stones, under a red sky.

'You can't scare me!' shouted Jake.

'Hahaha!' The old reindeer clapped his hooves again. 'How about THIS?'

The ground began to shake under Jake's feet. Something was stomping towards him. He looked around wildly and saw nothing, but the stomping grew louder, and there was a sound of distant chanting:

'*Bum-bum-bum-bum!*'

Out of nowhere, a crowd of huge, coloured dinosaurs came marching down the hill towards him.

Jake tried to run away from them, but this was the kind of dream where you can't run; he was stuck to the ground and the huge dinosaurs were so close that he could smell their breath, like hot rubber bands. The champion T-Rex with the blob of yellow on his head was at the front, and his blue mouth gaped open, bristling with bright blue teeth.

'HELP!' shouted Jake.

Just when he was sure he was about to be swallowed, a loud voice rang out, 'Dinos – SLEEP!'

And all at once the dinosaurs vanished.

Sadie stood beside him, wearing her favourite fairy dress over her pyjamas.

'Thanks, Sadie!' said Jake breathlessly. 'You saved me just in time – but what are you doing in my dream?'

'This isn't your dream,' said Sadie. 'It's **MINE!** How did you get into it?'

'Hahahaha!' cried the voice of Philpott. 'Let this be a lesson to you both!'

The bare hillside gave a great heave and the whole bleak dreamscape seemed to fold up around them. The two children were now in an endless white space. The only thing they could see in the emptiness was a flickering screen.

'I thought we were waking up,' said Sadie. 'Where are we?'

'I don't know,' said Jake. 'I think we're still dreaming, but I haven't a clue how to get out of it.'

'Maybe we should scream for Mum and Dad,' suggested Sadie. 'You know how loud my scream is.'

She opened her mouth and took a deep breath. Before she could let out one of her terrible screams, however, someone said:

'Hmm – that went well!'

Philpott's face appeared on the fuzzy screen. He

smiled and seemed to press a button that was just out of sight.

'Now what's next?' he muttered to himself. 'I suppose I should visit my nephew, before he eats up all his food.'

'Shhh!' hissed Jake. 'He thinks he's switched us off! He can't see us and he doesn't know we can see him — we can spy on him and find out where he's keeping Ginger!'

They watched Philpott on the screen, pottering about in what looked like a dark cave lit by one small lamp. He tidied up a few things on the floor and wrote something in a notebook with a hoof-pencil.

Jake sneezed; for a moment he was afraid he had given them away, but Philpott took absolutely no notice.

'Look at the time!' the rickety old reindeer said to himself. 'I'd better shave off twenty minutes!'

The fuzzy screen made it hard to see what Philpott was doing, but he seemed to be running backwards in small circles.

'Why is he running backwards?' asked Sadie.

'He thinks it reverses time,' said Jake.

'I hope this dream doesn't stop too soon,' said Sadie. 'We haven't seen anything useful yet.'

Philpott galloped until he was exhausted, and then he stopped to take a long, slurping drink of water from a metal bucket. Then he coughed a couple of times.

'Ready now,' said Philpott. 'Off to Regent's Park! FC thinks he's so clever – but he'll never guess where I've hidden Ginger!' He started to trot away and then turned back to stare into the camera. 'Mustn't waste the battery—'

The dream popped like a burst bubble and disappeared.

Jake was awake and back in his bed – and suddenly he knew exactly where Philpott had hidden Ginger.

'Mum, Dad! Call Father Christmas!' he shouted.

'Mum!' shrieked Sadie on the other side of the wall.

Together they cried out, 'Ginger's at **LONDON ZOO!**'

ELEVEN
Operation Rescue Ginger

'Well done, you two,' said Father Christmas. 'You've saved me a lot of work, and I'll make sure Philpott keeps out of your dreams in future.'

It was Sunday morning and the great man had come to the circus tent while the Trubshaws were still having breakfast. He was splendidly dressed in a suit of scarlet velvet trimmed with snow-white fur, and his dazzling white beard was neatly combed.

'My computer detected a faint magic signal at

London Zoo,' said Dad. 'It's definitely Ginger.'

'I'm off to rescue him now,' said FC. 'It's going to be rather tricky, and that's why I'm here – I need some human help.'

'I'll help!' said Jake eagerly.

'And me!' cried Sadie.

'You're too little,' said Mum. 'And Jake, it's too dangerous for you.'

'Actually,' said FC, 'I'm going to need **ALL** of you – including the children.'

'Why?'

'I'll explain while we're in the space shuttle.'

Mr and Mrs Trubshaw were doubtful, but Jake and Sadie were thrilled – especially Sadie, who was always complaining that she was never allowed to do anything exciting.

'Wait till I tell Belinda and the girls in my class!'

'There won't be any danger,' said FC, with a beaming smile. 'Now I must ask you all to remove your elf suits and change into your human clothes.'

'But what about you?' asked Jake.

'I won't need human clothes today,' said FC, with a

128

chuckle. 'You'll see why when we get there!'

Everyone hurried to put on their rather crumpled earth clothes, and when they were dressed a flying taxi whisked the Trubshaws to the airfield, where they boarded the shuttle. FC waited until they had taken off and were hurtling through space, and then he told them what he wanted them to do.

'Well, that seems pretty simple,' said Dad.

'It'll feel funny to pop back to earth,' said Mum. 'What time will it be when we get there?'

'The same time you left,' said FC. 'The weekend before the schools break up for Christmas.'

'But we'll be on earth for Christmas – what if we bump into ourselves?'

'It's too complicated to think about.' FC took a heap of coats from a locker. 'The weather will be cold, so I brought these.'

The coats were their own winter coats, usually hanging up in the hall at home.

'My pink puffa jacket!' squeaked Sadie. 'Where did that come from?'

'Your house, of course,' said FC. 'And you'll find your

coats there when you get back.'

Jake sniffed his blue coat and it smelt of home, which gave him a moment of wishing they were there – but this rescue mission was a million times more exciting.

'Here's your car key, Mrs Trubshaw,' said FC. 'You'll find your car outside the delivery entrance.'

'I don't think it's legal to park there,' said Mum. 'What if it's been towed away?'

'Oh, I can park anywhere I like, even if it's someone else's car,' said FC. 'It's one of the perks of being Father Christmas. Now put your coats on, everyone, and brace yourselves for the landing!'

It was very strange indeed to walk out of the space shuttle into the middle of London. The shuttle

vanished with a click of FC's fingers, and they were standing on a large patch of grass, shivering in the chilly December air. It was immediately obvious why FC had not needed to change into human clothes. There were lots of people heading for the zoo, and half of them were dressed up as Father Christmas.

'The zoo is having a special Christmas Fair,' FC explained. 'They want everybody to wear Santa costumes.'

'I've never seen so many Father Christmases in one place,' said Dad. 'You really blend in.'

'Except that your costume's much better than everyone else's,' said Sadie, taking FC's hand. 'And your beard isn't glued on.'

'This is awesome,' said Jake. 'Wouldn't everyone be amazed if they knew you were the **REAL** Father Christmas?'

'Thank you, my dear children.' FC gave Dad a large aerosol can and a silver whistle. 'David, you're the lookout. If anyone disturbs you, blow twice on this whistle. And spray this on the gates as soon as you see us.'

'OK,' said Dad. 'Good luck!'

Mr and Mrs Trubshaw hurried across the grass towards the zoo's delivery entrance.

'If anyone asks,' FC told Jake and Sadie, 'I'm your grandfather and we're just an ordinary family – OK?'

'OK!' said Jake, grinning because he was so excited. 'We remember the plan, don't we, Sadie?'

'Yes!' said Sadie. 'And I can't wait to do it!'

They joined the crowd of Father Christmases and nobody looked at them twice – as Dad had said, FC blended right in.

Sadie read the big notice they saw when they got inside the zoo. 'Christmas Fair This Way – Come and Meet the Reindeer.'

'They've borrowed a little herd of about twenty-five ordinary, non-magic reindeer,' said FC. 'They're in a big temporary stable, and that's where we'll find Ginger – what better place to hide him?'

Everyone wanted to see the reindeer. They had to queue outside the temporary shed, in a slow line of children and Santas. Inside the shed it was warm and smelt of hay and reindeer poo. A wire fence separated the people from the reindeer and the enclosure was guarded by two zookeepers.

The non-magic reindeer were very different from their friends on Yule-1. They were dumpier and clumsier, and their faces all looked the same.

'They're really sweet, even if they can't talk or fly,' said Sadie. 'I'd love to come and see them when we get home properly.'

Jake noticed something strange. The ordinary reindeer were moving towards FC's part of the fence. The great man smiled his kindest smile and reached over to stroke the nose of the nearest reindeer. He made a huffing sound, deep in his chest. The reindeer huffed back at him, and one of the others chipped in with what sounded like a cross between a bark and a cough.

'I learned to speak their language when I started to train my first squadrons,' said FC. 'This one says he's seen Ginger and Philpott. He says none of the reindeer like Philpott – apparently, he stole some of their food. And he says Ginger is tied up under the manger.'

'But how can we get to him?' Jake asked, looking helplessly at the long feeding trough filled with reindeer pellets. 'Everyone will see us!'

'These animals may not be magic,' said FC, 'but that doesn't mean they don't care about Christmas. They're going to help us by creating a diversion.'

It was a weird and wonderful sight. The herd of reindeer began to bray like angry donkeys and to run about inside their enclosure, bumping against each other and squashing together in a great, furry huddle.

The humans were shocked and alarmed, and several people screamed.

Jake whispered, 'We're ready, FC!'

'We remember everything you told us,' whispered Sadie.

Every eye was on the rioting reindeer, and nobody noticed when one of the Father Christmases jumped over the fence and moved the manger aside. FC was very old, but also super-strong. In less than a minute, he jumped out again, holding the prisoner in his arms.

'Ginger!' cried Sadie.

'Children – follow me!'

FC dashed out of the shed, with Jake and Sadie close behind him. Once again nobody noticed, thanks to the chaos created by the reindeer's diversion.

On the path outside, FC untied Ginger's legs and took the gag off his muzzle. Part of his Santa outfit was a sack marked 'GIFTS' and Jake and Sadie quickly pulled out the things inside it – a big grey coat, a tall black hat with a large brim, a pair of huge mittens and a pair of clumpy boots. Sadie put the mittens over Ginger's front hooves. Jake put the boots over his back hooves. FC hustled him into the coat and pulled the hat over his antlers. With the coat collar turned up and the brim of the hat pulled over his muzzle, and standing on his back legs, the young reindeer could just about pass as a very odd-looking human.

'Th-thank you!' croaked Ginger. 'Thank you! My uncle stole my Turbo-cake and hid me in this primitive place!'

'Where's Philpott now?' asked Jake. 'Is he hiding here too?'

'I don't know where he's hiding,' said Ginger. 'Somewhere on earth – you must stop him, FC – he brought a load of those tiny dinosaurs and he's trying to sell them to human shops!'

'I shouldn't worry,' said FC. 'Even a talking reindeer would have trouble doing that – unless he has a human helper.'

'But he DOES!' groaned Ginger. 'He's managed to hypnotise one of the zookeepers to help him when he's not on duty here. His name is Carl, and he's quite a nice guy really, but my uncle has programmed him to guard me, in case I try to escape.'

'We'd better get out as quickly as possible,' said FC, frowning. 'Children, you remember your instructions.'

FC held one of Ginger's front legs and Jake held the other, to make it easier for him to walk on his back legs. Sadie carried the empty sack and by the time the ordinary reindeer had calmed down, they were already hurrying away down the path.

'Well done, everyone!' said the real Father Christmas.

'HEY!' yelled a human voice behind them. 'One of the reindeer is missing!'

'I spoke too soon,' said FC. 'Keep walking.'

An alarm bell rang out and the crowd of humans began to chatter excitedly, and to mill about in all directions at once. Luckily, they were all looking for an escaped reindeer, and paid no attention to the weird-looking human in the huge black hat.

The walk was not long, but to Jake and Sadie it felt endless, and they were both very worried about getting caught. It was easier to hurry when FC led them off the main path and behind one of the zoo buildings, to the delivery entrance.

'There's Dad,' said Jake.

'And our car,' said Sadie.

As soon as he spotted them, Dad sprayed the tall metal gates with the can FC had given him. They swung open to reveal the Trubshaws' old green Volvo, with Mum sitting behind the wheel.

'Phew – I thought you'd never get here!' said Dad. 'We've already seen at least three police cars!'

'Nothing to worry about,' said FC. 'As I told you, I can park anywhere I like – and that applies to you when you're with me.'

'Hello, Mr Trubshaw,' Ginger said politely, from inside his hat. 'I can't thank you enough!'

'Don't mention it,' said Dad.

FC sat in front, next to Mum. Jake and Sadie scrambled into the boot and Dad sat in the back seat beside Ginger (Jake couldn't decide if the disguised reindeer looked less strange when he was sitting in a human car, or even stranger).

'STOP!' Just as Mum started the car, a young man in a peaked cap came dashing after them – it was Carl, the zookeeper Philpott had hypnotised. 'GIVE BACK THAT REINDEER!'

Father Christmas opened the window and blew softly in the young man's face.

'Where am I? What's going on?' Carl looked bewildered, as if he had just woken up.

'He will forget all about this,' said FC, closing the

window. 'Now follow the signs for the rose garden – and don't bother about the speed limit!'

The next few minutes were exciting and slightly scary. Mum put her foot down on the accelerator, and the car zoomed along the road so fast that the houses and trees were nothing but a blur.

'Turn left,' said FC.

Mum turned left, onto a path that was closed to traffic.

At first they saw nothing but grass and wintry rose bushes, and then the space shuttle appeared out of nowhere.

'Quick as you can, everyone!' said FC cheerfully.

Ginger shook off his disguise and galloped to the shuttle, followed closely by FC and the Trubshaws. In a matter of seconds they were strapped into their seats and the shuttle was hurtling away from the earth.

'I've never driven so fast in my life!' gasped Mum. 'What'll happen to our car?'

'I whisked your car away with a touch of magic, and it's already back outside your house,' said FC. 'Thank you, my dear humans – Operation Rescue Ginger has been a complete success.'

'I'm incredibly grateful,' said Ginger. 'The earth reindeer were nice enough, but I don't think they're interested in anything but food.'

'Wait a minute,' said Jake. 'Shouldn't we stay on earth to find Philpott?'

'His signal's not strong enough,' said Dad. 'I need to do more work on the Yule-1 computer.'

'Philpott's got a contact on Yule-1,' said Ginger. 'You won't find my uncle until you find the reindeer or elf who's working for him.'

FC gave a sigh and shook his head. 'But who would be wicked enough to work for Philpott? I can't believe one of my dear little creatures is a traitor!'

TWELVE
Contact

Lucy was waiting at the airfield, and when she saw her brother, she hugged him joyfully.

'Ginger – home and safe! Thank you, FC!' She kissed FC and all the Trubshaws. 'Thank you, brave humans!'

Jake and Sadie grinned at each other; the kisses were a bit furry and slobbery, but it was nice to be called 'brave'.

'I'd better go straight to head office to start work,' said Dad. 'I wish I had my elf suit – my human trousers are too tight.'

'Good luck,' said Mum. 'We'll try to have a quiet afternoon, after all that excitement.'

'But I LIKE excitement,' said Sadie. 'It's not fair when Jake gets it all.'

'You were pretty good,' said Jake kindly.

Back in Poffle Glen, they told the Prancers about their adventure. Sadie and Belinda then shut themselves in Belinda's bedroom, to play yet another mysterious new game.

'Let's play "Delivery Wars 4",' Jake said to Percy. 'We don't have that on earth, and I've missed it.'

'Great!' said Percy. 'I'll get my hoof-adaptors – and then I'll thrash you!'

'That's what you think!'

Jake's weekend had been thrilling, but though he loved adventures he had to admit he was glad to have a restful time just playing with his reindeer friend.

He didn't know that he was about to make a major breakthrough.

* * *

On Monday morning, they walked into their classroom to find a different teacher – an old, stout lady reindeer with round glasses and a kind face.

'Hello, everyone! My name is Mrs Ethel Donner, and I'll be teaching you while Mr Comet is away.'

'What happened to Mr Comet?' asked Jake. 'Is he ill?'

'I'm afraid poor Mr Comet is at home, under house arrest,' said Mrs Donner. 'He surprised his girlfriend with a huge shower of pink rose petals last night, and it blocked all the drains in her street. The neighbours wanted him locked up for being a public nuisance – but of course, there are no prisons here.'

'Primrose must've been really embarrassed,' Percy said during morning break, when he and Jake were in the playground with Fred and Eric. 'That's worse than the brass band.'

'I know this sounds a bit mean,' said Fred, with his mouth full of chomp-nuts. 'But I don't get why Mr Comet is so crazy about an ordinary-looking reindeer like Primrose Cupid.'

'I'm an elf, so I don't know much about reindeer beauty,' said Eric. 'All the same, I do think it's strange that he believes she's so incredibly gorgeous – it's as if she's cast a spell on him!'

'A spell?' Jake remembered again what he had seen at the warehouse, and something in his mind suddenly clicked into place. 'Of course! Eric, can I borrow your phone? I have to call my dad at head office!'

'We're not allowed to use our phones during school hours,' said Percy. 'Unless it's an emergency.'

'This is an emergency – I know who it is!' Jake grabbed Eric's elf phone. 'I've found **PhiLpott's CONTACT!**'

* * *

'Nice work, human boy,' said Professor Rudolf.

'Yes, indeed,' said Father Christmas. 'Thank you for coming into the office at such short notice.'

A few minutes after he had made his phone call, a police car had arrived at the school to whisk Jake, Percy and Fred to head office.

'Excuse me, FC,' said Percy. 'Why do you need me and Fred?'

'You three are all part of my special squadron, the

History Makers,' said FC. 'Last time Jake came to Yule-1, the History Makers helped to defeat Krampus and save Christmas.'

'And now Christmas must be saved again,' said Mr Trubshaw. 'I designed a magic future-casting app, and found some very disturbing pictures of what could happen in the future, if we don't stop Philpott selling his terrible inventions on earth.'

The human boy and the two small reindeer stared at the big screen behind FC's desk and saw a series of very odd images – huge, coloured dinosaurs crushing buildings, and famous people who had turned blue.

'Thanks to Jake's sharp eyes,' said FC, 'we've found the reindeer who's helping Philpott on this planet.' He pressed a button under his desk and, a moment later, two police reindeer came into the office with their prisoner. Primrose was in heavy hoof-cuffs, and as soon as she saw Father Christmas, she cried, 'Please don't blame Clarence! Yes, I was working for Philpott, but Clarence didn't know and none of this is his fault! I didn't mean to ruin Christmas!'

'You'd better tell us the whole story,' said FC, stern but kind. 'How on earth did a nice reindeer like you get mixed up with a character like Philpott?'

Primrose hung her head and said, in a very small voice, 'He gave me Love-drops.'

There was a long silence. Everyone – including FC – was baffled, until Professor Rudolf suddenly let out a chuckle.

'Of course – Love-drops! It's another of Philpott's terrible inventions!'

'They're pills,' said Primrose miserably. 'You give them to people to make them fall in love with you.' She looked at Jake. 'Be honest, human boy – you were surprised when you saw me, and you wondered why Clarence Comet thought I was so divinely beautiful.'

'Well – er . . .' began Jake, not wanting to hurt her feelings.

'The truth is I've been putting Philpott's Love-drops into Clarence's hot chocolate every day. They made him think I was very beautiful.'

'But of course, it all went wrong,' said Rudolf, still chuckling. 'As all his silly inventions do!'

Primrose nodded miserably. 'It was great at first, but then the Love-drops worked too well and the love songs started – and the orchestras – and the firework display that blew my parents out of bed – and now he's under house arrest and it's all my fault! I know I shouldn't have given him the pills, and I'm sorry now, but I don't want him to find out that I'm UGLY!'

FC patted her neck. 'But my dear little reindeer, you're not ugly! I know you didn't mean to be naughty, and if you hand over those Love-drops, we'll say no more about it.' He gently took the cuffs off her hooves.

'OK,' said Primrose. She took a bottle of pills from a pocket on her collar and dropped it on FC's desk. 'Will Clarence still like me a bit after they've worn off?'

'Of course he will!' said FC firmly.

'Now let's get down to business,' croaked Rudolf. 'Young lady, do you know the whereabouts of Philpott?'

'No – I swear!' said Primrose. 'He never gave me an address. I don't even know what planet he's on.'

'I thought he was on earth,' said Jake.

'All he told me was that he was hiding out in a glass castle on a dinosaur island.'

'That sounds like something out of a fairy story,' said Jake's dad. 'There's nothing like that on earth.'

'Dad – don't you remember?' Jake was so excited that he jumped out of his chair. 'We saw an island that had dinosaurs on it!'

'Don't be silly,' said Dad. 'You're letting your imagination run away with you.'

'They weren't real dinosaurs – they were statues in a park, and we saw them when we went to visit Auntie Diane.'

Father Christmas let out a great rumble of laughter. 'Jake, you're on fire today! David, make a deep search of South London, and pay special attention to a place called **CRYSTAL PALACE!**'

Dad bent over his keyboard and his fingers worked busily. 'Good grief – that's his "glass castle"! I was all set to sweep the whole of planet earth for a signal, and that silly old reindeer is hiding in a rainy London park!'

'Now we know where he is,' said FC, 'let's go and fetch him.'

'Wait a moment,' said Professor Rudolf. 'You can't spare one of your squadrons without messing up all the Christmas deliveries.'

'This is just the job for my special squadron.' FC stood up, tall and magnificent in his scarlet suit. 'The History Makers!'

'Cool – we're flying again!' Jake high-fived Percy's hoof.

'Uh-oh,' said Fred. 'My mum's not going to like this.'

THIRTEEN
Flying Again

'I've brought his woolly vest and his antler-cosy,' said Mrs Dancer. 'And his warm bottom-cover.'

'Mum!' hissed Fred. 'Stop embarrassing me!'

'Honestly, Mrs Dancer,' said Father Christmas. 'Fred won't need any extra clothes.'

'But he's such a DELICATE little reindeer, FC, and those space winds will go straight to his chest!'

Fred, Jake and Percy were in a large hangar at the airfield and their parents had come to wave them off and wish them luck.

'Do stop fussing, Eileen,' said Fred's dad. 'FC's flying reindeer don't wear bottom-covers.'

Percy's mum gave Mrs Dancer a friendly nuzzle. 'I'm nervous too – but you know they'll be safe with FC!'

Jake's mother hugged him. 'Please be careful!'

A team of elves were busily preparing the reindeer's harnesses, saddlebags and nose-lights (Jake wore his lights on a specially adapted hat).

'Attention, reindeer!' called FC. 'You all know why you're here. You are my emergency squadron. And though I ride on all my sleighs in spirit, today I shall be joining you in person. Our objective is to capture Philpott without disrupting the Christmas deliveries. We'll be harnessing up as soon as you've had your Turbo-cakes.'

'Excuse me, FC.' Tolly Blobb tugged at FC's long red robe. 'What about the change to the line-up?'

'Oh, yes,' said FC. 'Harriet Donner is away on her honeymoon, so I've chosen Primrose Cupid to fly in her place.'

Primrose trotted into the hangar, looking very small

and shy. 'Are you sure I can do this, FC?'

'Of course you can do it, my brave little reindeer!' said Father Christmas, with a beaming smile. 'You did very well in all your flying exams at school.'

'But what about the Love-drops?'

'You didn't mean any harm – I know you're not on Philpott's side, and this will be just the thing to boost your confidence.' The great man patted Primrose's head.

That was one of the nicest things about Yule-1, Jake thought: if anyone did something wrong, they were forgiven immediately.

'Welcome to our special squadron,' said Lucy Blitzen, giving Primrose a hug.

All the other History Makers gathered round the brave volunteer reindeer – Ginger and Dasher from the Jambusters, so handsome in their RAF moustaches, Algernon Comet in his 3Rs rasta hat, and Jake and Percy.

Fred gave her the biggest hug of all. 'Don't be nervous – if I can pull a sleigh, **ANYBODY** can!'

It was time to prepare for take-off. There were final

hugs and kisses, and all the parents left the hangar. Jake was incredibly excited, with butterflies in his stomach, and he saw that Percy felt the same.

'Mmm – something smells **DELICIOUS!**' cried Primrose.

'Those are the Turbo-cakes,' said FC. 'So that you can breathe in space.'

Two elves appeared, pushing a large trolley filled with the sticky, smelly black cakes.

'I didn't know they tasted so yummy!' Primrose ate her cake with such a big smile that her small eyes sparkled and she suddenly looked very pretty.

'Yuck!' shuddered Jake.

All reindeer adored the taste of Turbo-cakes, but they were not designed for humans and Jake thought they tasted even more disgusting than tinned moss. He knew how important they were, however, and bravely ate the cake FC gave him. For a moment he felt sick and was sure he was going to throw up – but just like last time, the sickness wore off quickly and his body was filled with super-strength.

'Wow!' He drew a deep breath. 'This feels fantastic!'

'HELP!' Primrose – still licking her lips – had shot up into the air. 'Oh dear, I haven't done this since school! I've forgotten how to get down again!'

'That's just what keeps happening to me,' said Fred.

Lucy grabbed one of Primrose's hooves and pulled her down to the ground. 'It'll soon come back to you.'

'I'm afraid I can't give you more time to practise,' said FC. 'My elves are waiting to fit you into your harness.'

'A real red harness!' gasped Primrose, her furry face radiant as the elves clipped the straps of scarlet leather around her. 'I never dreamed this would happen to me!'

'You look very smart,' said Jake.

'It suits you,' said Percy.

The squadron was now ready. The seven reindeer and one human put on their nose-lights and went out to the airfield, where FC's special sleigh was waiting on the grass.

'History Makers, we have an exciting time ahead,' said FC. 'When we get to earth it will be Christmas Eve and I will be delivering a sleigh-full of presents in the Sydenham area of South London.'

'We'll be part of a real delivery!' muttered Percy, his black reindeer eyes gleaming with excitement. **'Oh, CRUMBS!'**

'When we've delivered the presents, we'll proceed to the park at Crystal Palace,' said FC. 'And then we'll give Philpott the surprise of his life! As you all know, **CHRISTMAS** is about a lot more than expensive gifts and fancy food. It's a time of good thoughts and kind actions, when the whole world is filled with **LIGHT** and **HOPE**. I expect all my reindeer – and my human – to have hearts filled with **PEACE** and **GOODWILL**.'

FC nodded to his elves and they fastened the History Makers into their places in front of the sleigh. Jake took a couple of steps in his leg-straps, to make sure he would be able to prance in time with the reindeer.

FC patted all his reindeer and shook hands with Jake. He climbed into his sleigh, and cried out in a voice that boomed across the airfield –

'Now, DASHER,
Now, GINGER,
Now, PRIMROSE and DANCER!
On, LUCY,
On, COMET,
On, TRUBSHAW and PRANCER!
To the top of the porch! To the top of the wall!
Now dashaway! Dashaway! Dashaway all!'

There was a great gust of wind; the air roared in their ears. Jake remembered the superfast speed of FC's sleigh, which made his hands and feet tingle. For a few seconds he thought they were going to crash into the painted sky, but a trapdoor opened and the sleigh shot through it into outer space.

FOURTEEN
Dinosaur Island

Jake had been fascinated by outer space since he was little, and he wanted to stare at the amazing sights they passed – the clouds of glittering dust, the shooting stars, the beautiful planets that were coloured like birds' eggs – but he had to concentrate on his prancing.

'Nice exit, reindeer,' said the voice of FC in their earpieces. 'Stardust storm ahead – shields up!'

The invisible shields made a kind of bubble around FC and his reindeer, which protected them from the storm. A cloud of golden glitter swallowed them; Jake could see nothing and had to make an effort to prance in time with the rest of the team. The cloud fell away behind them and Jake saw how fast they were zipping across the universe.

For the first ten minutes he didn't recognise any of the planets, and then a cluster of lights up ahead got brighter and brighter and turned into the Milky Way. A few minutes later they entered his own solar system, which he knew very well from the poster on his bedroom wall.

'Earth's moon coming up,' said FC's voice. 'Brace yourselves for the atmosphere!'

A moment later the sleigh crashed through the atmosphere of earth, and Jake was back on his own planet. The air felt different on his skin and it was freezing cold – he remembered that this was NEXT Christmas Eve, and if he flew to his own house, he'd find himself asleep in bed – but this was too confusing to think about for long.

'We're invisible to humans now,' said FC's voice. 'But not to animals, so do your best not to frighten people's pets; remember that one little glimpse of you can set a dog barking for hours.'

'That was SO exciting!' said Primrose. 'I should've chosen flight training when I finished school, instead of warehouse work – but I thought I wasn't trendy enough to be in a real squadron.'

'That's rubbish!' said Lucy. 'All the squadrons will want you after this. You should join the Janiacs – you'd look lovely in our blue bonnet.'

'Attention, reindeer!' said FC. 'We're switching to **DELIVERY SPEED!**'

The sleigh paused in mid-air for a split second, as if holding its breath, and then it shot forwards at incredible speed. Jake had never moved so fast; this was a hundred times faster than the fastest theme-park ride.

This is how the wind feels, he thought.

He knew he would never forget this – he was actually helping FC to deliver Christmas presents. The sleigh flashed through the streets of South London, and Jake saw the insides of the houses and blocks of flats like a speeded-up film – Christmas trees, stockings, strings of lights, sleeping children.

He didn't know how long it lasted.

The sleigh slowed down. Jake could breathe normally again. He nudged Percy, prancing along beside him. 'Are you OK, Perce?'

'I'm not sure,' gasped Percy. 'I thought my ears were going to blow off!'

The sleigh stopped on a wide piece of grass beside a lake.

'This is the place,' said Jake. 'The statues are on an island in the lake.' Though it was very dark, he could just make out the black outlines of the famous dinosaur statues.

'Well done, everyone,' said Father Christmas. 'We'll stop here for our break; we're still invisible to humans.'

The reindeer and Jake unfastened their harnesses.

'Phew!' gasped Primrose. 'My antlers are all in a whirl!'

'We've got loads of snacks this year.' Lucy trotted over with a large bag of apples, raw carrots, mince pies, chocolate biscuits and all the other treats that the people of Sydenham had left for the reindeer. 'Help yourselves!'

Jake chose
a slightly squashed
mince pie and Percy and Fred chomped
their way through a heap of raw carrots. Father
Christmas ate the cheese and biscuits that someone had
left for him, washed down with a small gin and tonic.

'I'm glad to see how much humans love my reindeer!'
said FC. 'Now that the presents have been delivered,
our special mission begins. I want you all to climb over
those railings and surround the island in the lake. And
keep quiet – don't give Philpott any clue that we're here.'

The railings were tall and sharp, but Jake was super-
strong from the Turbo-cake, and jumping over felt as
easy as bouncing on a trampoline. The seven reindeer
and one human spread out around the lake with the
small, dark island in the middle, totally silent except
for one small splash when Fred tripped over his hooves
and fell into the water.

It was strange to see the dinosaur statues at night,
crouched amongst the thick bushes and shrubs. The
stillness and silence were so deep that Jake started to
wonder if FC had brought them to the wrong place.

But then he heard a rustling sound in the bushes, and the snap of someone treading on a branch.

'PHILPOTT   BLITZEN!' called FC. 'You're surrounded – come out and give yourself up!'

'Pooh!' said a voice somewhere on the island.

'Don't be ridiculous!' said Father Christmas, stern but kind. 'This is no place for you.'

'It's YOUR fault!' snapped the voice of Philpott. 'You should never have sacked me from the toy factory! I've come to earth to sell my Tino-saurs to people who'll

APPRECIATE them!'

'He **HAD** to sack you!' Primrose called out. 'Your inventions are dangerous!'

'Is that Primrose Cupid? Well, of all the ingratitude! I let you have my wonderful Love-drops.'

The branches moved and Jake saw the outline of antlers. Philpott let out a screech. Every bush on the island began to toss and heave – and suddenly, the statues were real dinosaurs, lumbering towards them through the water.

Before anyone had time to panic, however, FC calmly raised his hand. In a few seconds, the dinosaurs were statues again.

'Come on, Philpott, no more tricks,' he said patiently. 'You know you can't stay here! My special flying reindeer aren't designed to live with humans.'

The branches were very still now; Philpott was hiding again.

'Uncle Phil!' called Lucy. 'Please come home!'

'NO!' yelled the voice of Philpott. **'YOU'LL neveR catch me!'**

There was a blaze of white light, so bright that Jake had to screw up his eyes, and a violent gust of wind that blew them all (except FC) off their feet.

With a great clattering and rumbling, a small spaceship shot out of the bushes – a spaceship that seemed to be made of cereal packets, sticky tape and tinfoil, and which wobbled alarmingly. Jake thought it looked like a cross between a rickety kite and something Sadie had made at school.

It zoomed away into space, and Jake and the reindeer stared after it.

'I didn't think Philpott was clever enough to build his own rocket,' said Percy.

'He's **NOT!**' groaned Lucy. 'Please help him, FC – that contraption will fall apart and then he'll be lost in space!'

'No need to worry,' said FC. 'Philpott forgot to switch off his microchip. We'll pick him up on the way home. Harnesses on, History Makers – we're going on a **SPACE CHASE!**'

'Cool!' said Jake.

'Oh, wow!' gasped Percy.

'Oh, help!' squeaked Fred.

'You mustn't be scared,' said Primrose. 'This is the most exciting thing that's ever happened to me!'

In a few minutes, all the reindeer were safely harnessed.

'Attention, History Makers!' FC climbed into his seat. 'This will be no normal journey back to Yule-1. We will not be sticking to the usual paths. You must all be ready to make quick jumps and swerves to stay on Philpott's trail – and don't let him hurt himself. He's not nearly as magic as he thinks.' He picked up the reins. 'One – two – three – squadron – DASHAWAY!'

FIFTEEN
Space Chase

The sleigh soared into the sky, and the lights of London fell away behind them. Jake braced himself for the bump as they went through the earth's atmosphere, and they were back in the mysterious hugeness of space.

'Ouch!' said Percy, prancing beside him. 'A bit of rubbish nearly hit me in the eye!'

Jake risked a quick look at his friend. 'It's stuck in your antlers now.'

'What is it?'

'I don't know.' He took another
quick look. 'I think it's tinfoil, and there's
a bit of cardboard that says "Weetabix".'

'OUCH!' shouted the voice of Dasher in
his earpiece. 'I just got hit by an egg box – watch out
for floating rubbish, everyone!'

'Philpott's home-made rocket is breaking up,' said
FC's voice. 'But I've still got his signal, so he can't have
gone very far.'

The sleigh made a sudden swerve and shot away in a
new direction, so incredibly fast that Jake's feet nearly
lost their prancing rhythm. They dived and dodged in
the darkness, past strange lumps of rock and through
hailstorms of tiny meteors. He was concentrating hard,
and didn't see the missile until it hit them.

The missile – a smoking, dirty, sooty, smelly ball of rubbish – smashed violently into the sleigh.

'Attention, reindeer,' cried Father Christmas. 'We're under attack and my invisible shield is broken! Keep on prancing, as fast as you can!'

Jake was terrified, but somehow managed to carry on prancing. More rubbish-bombs whistled past them and over their heads, and then another one hit the sleigh with a great SPLAT.

'We'll have to make an emergency landing on the moon,' said FC. 'That hasn't happened for more than four hundred earth years!'

'The moon!' gasped Jake. 'We're landing on the moon!' He had dreamed about this ever since he was small.

It was a short, bumpy, scary ride – and then FC's damaged sleigh stopped in a vast, flat, rocky desert that stretched as far as the eye could see.

'Good thing I remembered to bring a can of gravity spray!' FC sprayed the sleigh and the squadron with instant gravity. 'This will stop us floating away.'

The seven reindeer and single human were all out of breath. FC told them to rest for a few minutes and they wriggled out of their harnesses to stretch their legs on the moon's bare surface.

The gleaming red sleigh was dented and there was a jagged hole at the back.

'Not too much damage,' said FC. 'I can easily patch it up.'

'Look!' shouted Ginger, pointing at a black shape in the pallid moonlight above their heads. 'It's Uncle Phil!'

The skinny old reindeer was covered with scraps of rubbish left over from his home-made rocket. 'Hahahaha – this moon belongs to ME now!'

'Philpott!' called FC. 'Please stop being so silly!'

'NO!'

The rocky ground began to shake underneath Jake's trainers.

Thump-thump-THUMP!

A cloud of moondust appeared on the horizon, getting closer and closer and bigger and bigger. Bright colours appeared through the dust. A crowd of

huge, plastic dinosaurs, all growling, was marching towards them.

All at once Jake remembered his dream. As loudly as he could, he yelled, 'Dinos – SLEEP!'

Nothing happened. The great creatures carried on lumbering towards them.

'W-why won't they stop?' gasped Percy.

'They only listen to Sadie – and she's not here!'

'Thank you, Jake.' Father Christmas took his mobile phone from the pocket of his scarlet suit. In the weird, windy moon silence, everyone could hear it ringing in Poffle Glen. 'Hello, Mrs Trubshaw, sorry to bother you. Could you ask Sadie to stop a large mob of plastic dinosaurs?'

He held up the phone and Sadie's voice cried, **'Dinos – SLEEP!'**

The dinosaurs stopped at once and dropped to the ground.

'Well done, Sadie,' said FC. 'And thank you for your help.' He switched off his phone with a cheerful smile and took his emergency toolbox out of the sleigh.

'Uncle Phil,' called Lucy. 'I know you're not really

wicked! Please let FC capture you before your Turbo-cake runs out!'

'**POOH!**' roared Philpott.

Jake saw that Philpott was struggling. His skinny old legs were paddling, but his voice was getting weaker and he was drifting like a leaf.

'I've had an idea,' he whispered, while FC began to mend the sleigh. 'If someone distracts him, me and Percy can make a grab for him.'

'I'll do it,' whispered Primrose. 'Take off your harnesses, boys!'

As quickly and quietly as possible, Jake unfastened the red harness (this was one time his human hands were very useful).

Primrose flew up through the thin moon atmosphere to Philpott. 'I've had enough of you! Stop being so mean – or I'll shake you till your antlers rattle!'

'Ha! You can't shake me, you weedy little lovesick reindeer!'

'Don't you call me names, you smelly old criminal!'

'**GO!**' yelled Jake.

He grabbed Percy's hoof and Fred's collar and

the three of them took a tremendous jump into the atmosphere. Jake snatched hold of Philpott's antlers, Fred seized his front leg and Percy repeated his successful biting of the old reindeer's bum.

'Ho-ho-ho!' roared Father Christmas. 'Nice work, everyone! Primrose, I knew it was a good idea to bring you.'

'You'll have to join a proper squadron now,' said Lucy. 'You're too talented for your job at the warehouse.'

'We could really use you in the Jambusters,' said Dasher. 'If you don't mind wearing a moustache.'

FC – still chuckling – tied up Philpott's legs and put him in the empty sleigh. 'When you've had your therapy and stopped being such an old twit, I might give you back your job in the toy factory.'

'Really?' Philpott's face lit up. 'That would be a dream come true!'

'It's nice to have you back, Uncle Phil,' said Ginger.

'Sorry I kidnapped you,' mumbled Philpott.

FC finished repairing the worst of the damage to the sleigh and fastened his seven reindeer (and one human) back into their harnesses.

Jake asked, 'What about the dinosaurs?'

The huge dinosaurs lay about like deflated balloons.

'I have plans for those dinosaurs, I'll send a team to pick them up,' said FC. 'Squadron – **DASHAWAY!**'

SIXTEEN
Reindeer Wedding

The flight back to Yule-1 was very happy and jolly. FC led a sing-song of 'We Wish You a Merry Christmas' and even Philpott joined in – Jake suspected he was relieved not to be wicked any more, especially as he wasn't very good at it.

FC had called the airfield as soon as they left the moon, and they arrived home to a cheering crowd of reindeer and elves. The sleighs that were taking off did fancy loop the loops in mid-air.

'I can see my mum!' Fred pointed to a stout reindeer who was holding up a sign: 'WELCOME HOME, FREDDY-WEDDY!'

Jake saw his parents and Sadie in the crowd, waving excitedly as the sleigh landed on the grass.

'Look, Primrose!' cried Lucy. 'It's your boyfriend!'

There was Clarence Comet, holding a huge bunch of pink flowers.

'The Love-drops have worn off,' said FC, smiling. 'But it doesn't seem to have made much difference to his feelings!'

Clarence galloped over to kiss Primrose and give her the flowers. 'I didn't need any magic drops to love you,' he told her. 'You're wonderful without magic, and the prettiest reindeer on this or any other planet – will you marry me right now?'

'Oh – !' Primrose was so happy that she couldn't speak.

'I'm sorry about those dinosaurs,' said Philpott. 'I should never have trained them just to fight and say "bum". I'm afraid I don't know what to do with them now.'

'Where's Sadie?' Father Christmas asked, smiling at

the crowd.

'Here I am!' cried Sadie. 'Please, FC – everyone's nasty to the dinos, but they're really sweet if you're kind to them!'

'I know that now,' said FC. 'You and Belinda have shown me exactly how to deal with them, thanks to your new game.'

'New game?' Mum was puzzled. 'I thought you'd cleared up all those bits of paper.'

'This is different,' said Sadie. 'We've been designing a special dinosaur theme park. I drew them a lovely big swimming pool, and a cafe filled with peanut butter—'

'And I drew them a roller coaster!' said Belinda.

'It's a brilliant idea,' said FC. 'I'm going to build your theme park in the mountains. When the little creatures have been retrained, I shall open it to the public.'

The faces of the two seven-year-olds beamed with joy and they did their special hand-and-hoofshake.

'And now,' said FC, 'let's have a wedding!'

A crowd of elves ran onto the airfield, pushing long tables filled with fancy food and drink and an enormous white wedding cake. A crowd of reindeer appeared, with a beautiful arch made of flowers.

'Oh, I love weddings!' said Mrs Dancer, in the middle of covering Fred's face with kisses.

'Sadie and Belinda,' said Primrose, 'will you be my bridesmaids?'

'Oh – yes please!' gasped Sadie.

'I've always wanted to be a bridesmaid!' cried Belinda.

It was a beautiful wedding. Mr Comet chose his old friend Krampus to be his best man; the formerly wicked monster looked very proud with flowers in his shaggy black fur. Belinda and Sadie carried bunches of pink lilies and the bride wore yellow primroses in her antlers.

Father Christmas performed the ceremony, and the crowd of elves and reindeer burst into loud cheers. There was delicious food, reindeer champagne and dancing. Jake and Percy danced until they were dizzy. Fred danced while holding a huge slice of reindeer wedding cake. Ginger Blitzen made everyone laugh when he dressed up in his 'human' disguise.

'My dear Trubshaws,' said FC, 'you've all been magnificent and I can't thank you enough.'

Jake had been incredibly happy but now his heart sank. 'We're going home, aren't we?'

'Oh, **NO!**' cried Percy. 'You can't go yet!'

'It's time you returned to your proper lives, on your home planet.'

'But I won't get to see my theme park!' said Sadie.

'Oh, I think you will,' said FC. 'I have a feeling you'll be coming back to Yule-1, though I don't know when – or why.'

Jake didn't feel so sad now that he knew he would see Percy again. He hugged his best reindeer friend. 'Take care, Perce!'

'Take care, Jake!' said Percy.

'Try to come back in time for my next birthday,' said Fred. 'My mum says I can have my party somewhere really cool and dangerous!'

'We've had a very interesting visit,' said Dad. 'Will you be wiping our memories again?'

'Yes,' said FC. 'Grown-ups just can't handle the truth about Christmas. Jake and Sadie will remember everything; they're still young enough to understand.'

'I suppose that's best,' said Mum.

'There's just one more thing I must do.' FC picked up what looked like a large fire extinguisher. 'To make sure there's no more Badwill on my Christmas planet, I shall spray it with my special GOODWILL GLITTER!'

He held up the fire extinguisher and the air suddenly filled with a blizzard of shimmering golden glitter that made everyone feel kind and Christmassy –

***

And when the glitter cleared away, the Trubshaws were in their own kitchen on their own planet.

'It's the same time we left,' said Jake, looking around and feeling very glad to be back home. 'We haven't missed Christmas!'

'We've still got the last week of school before the holidays,' said Sadie. 'I'd better practise my hazelnut dance.'

'I'll put the decorations box back in the loft,' said Dad. 'Doesn't our tree look lovely?'

'And I'll make us some supper,' said Mum. 'I don't know why, but I feel as if I've just been to a big party!'

'Me too,' said Jake.

The air of home felt good on his skin and he realised how much he had missed his own planet. He didn't care about school on Monday, or even the fact that he